I0691460

Forever May Not Be Long Enough

Legends of the Romanorum, Volume 7

Mychael Black and Shayne Carmichael

Published by Arian Derwydd Books, LLC, 2024.

Legends of the Romanorum, Book 7

An ancient force has awakened and is hellbent on nothing short of the total destruction of the Romanorum. Mael Black and Cian Carmichael are thrust into the middle of things, and it's ultimately on their shoulders to save the Romanorum itself. In the meantime, they've got their hands full with bringing a new son into their family, and Mael's father trying to force Mael to denounce his relationship with Cian. Betrayals and violent court intrigue set the stage for what promises to be an epic end to Mael and Cian's story. But it's only the beginning for others.

Chapter One

Prince Mael Black carefully warded the room, insuring none outside would hear anything discussed. Whatever was in the wind, Diocourides didn't want it known. Mael settled, at ease, in one of the comfortable leather chairs beside Cian. "It shouldn't be too long. He mentioned nine o'clock."

"Do you have any idea what this is about?" Cian asked. "Whatever it is, it's under tight wraps."

"I haven't the first clue, but when Diocourides commands my attention, I have no choice but to listen."

"You could always ignore me, you know," Diocourides said as he walked through the door. "It's not like I'll stake you and leave you out to dry." Mael hastily stood and bowed. Dio waved his hand nonchalantly at Mael. "Do sit down and relax, my boy."

Cian smiled. "Good evening, Diocourides."

"A pleasure to see you again, Cian." Dio helped himself to one of the bottles of wine, pouring a glass before he took a chair.

"How are you this evening?" Cian asked him.

"That depends on how well you two react to the news I have for you." While Dio appeared relaxed, a near imperceptible tension began to show in him.

Mael's brow arched. "You know I will not argue with you."

"This time I'll unfortunately have to hold you to that, Mael. It concerns the Inferi Brotherhood and both of you."

Cian sat up a little straighter. "What about them?"

"Triarius' son, Aldrich, was behind a number of the problems with the weres. Aldrich has been dealt with, of course, but we've yet to find all of his followers. However..." Diocourides eyed them both. "Aldrich is Brandon's Father." When no reaction came, the elder vampire narrowed his gaze on Mael. "You are not required to be polite at this point."

"What?" Cian sank back into his seat, face pale. "His Father?"

Mael kept his own reaction hidden, knowing Cian would be stunned enough for the both of them. "It means quite a lot in terms of what Brandon is due and his responsibilities. Is Triarius going to demand his rights?"

"No, my son only wants to talk to Brandon. If the child wishes to take his place, I'll allow him to, Mael, but it's entirely up to him."

"Wait." Cian looked between them. "What place? What am I missing?"

"Triarius is a first formula, Cian," Mael said. "He is Diocourides' son. Therefore, Brandon is Diocourides' great-grandson. His place is in Rome as part of the Inner Circle. He is considerably more important than a stray we took in." Mael returned his attention to Diocourides. "Triarius is being generous, not demanding his rights. I'm surprised."

"He's aware Brandon is well taken care of, Mael. He simply wants to speak with the boy." Dio sipped his wine, appearing to be more of his usual, better-humored self.

"What about Triarius?" Cian asked. "Isn't this the same man who created the Brotherhood? Who walked out of the Romanorum? Are we certain he won't try to take Brandon from Cornelius?"

"He would be well within the law to do so if he chose, but apparently he isn't." Mael rested his hand over Cian's, giving his angel a faint smile. "If he wanted Brandon now, he would take him."

"Mael is quite right. My son isn't interested in raising Brandon, but I believe he wants the child to know where he comes from and to possibly leave the lines of communication between them open."

Cian let out a slow breath. "Does Cornelius know any of this? Does Brandon even know?"

"Your magician probably realizes Brandon is first formula," Diocourides said, glancing at Mael, "but little else. I doubt Brandon knows anything."

"I'm not thrilled with the idea, but I have to admit it is Triarius' and Brandon's right to know each other," Mael said. "I've not said anything about the headache of accepting the Brotherhood members into our society, Diocourides, but I understand your desire to do so."

"So when does Brandon find out? What is normally expected of a first formula, and will he be required to do whatever it is?" Cian asked.

"Some of those answers will have to be determined by Brandon himself. I suggest we call him in and explain it to him." Mael sent out a silent summons to his mage and Brandon. "I assume Triarius is somewhere nearby?"

"He's been waiting until I filled you in," Dio said. "He isn't the most... public sort of person."

"This should be interesting," Cian muttered.

A few moments later, the door opened and Brandon walked in, Cornelius behind him. "What's going on?" Brandon asked. "Cornelius said... oh..." He grinned at Dio. "Hi, Diocourides. Man, this must be important if it brought you all the way from Rome."

The moment Cornelius met Mael's steady gaze, a multitude of questions seemed poised on the mage's lips. Mael just shook his head slightly. "Diocourides is here to speak to you, Brandon."

Dio raised his hand, inviting the young vampire to sit in the empty seat near him. "Certain things have come to my attention that you need to know about."

Brandon sat down slowly. "Okay..." Cornelius took up residence behind Brandon, resting his hand on Brandon's shoulder.

Dio glanced up at the magician, giving him a reassuring look before he spoke again. "We know who created you, Brandon. His name was Aldrich, and he was the son of my son, Triarius. It changes your position a great deal from being a rogue, young man."

Brandon looked like someone had punched him in the gut. "What?" He shot a quick look over at Mael and Cian, then reached up and gripped Cornelius' hand. "How... ?"

Mael carefully watched Cornelius and Brandon both. Not by a flutter of a lash did the mage reveal he might have known anything. Cornelius' hand tightened around Brandon's.

"There's no reason to be afraid of anything, either of you," Dio continued. "I make no claims on Brandon, though he is my great-grandson, and neither will his grandfather. Triarius wishes to speak to Brandon, but other than that, he'll make no demands."

"What does first formula mean exactly?" Brandon asked.

"Many of the first formulas who reside in Rome are part of the Inner Circle. Some choose to live independently, but a few like the power." A wry smile creased Dio's lips. "Something I don't think interests you quite yet."

Brandon shook his head quickly. "No. No power. I'll stick to magic. When do I get to meet my grandfather?"

Dio chuckled as he motioned toward the door along the back wall. A pocket of shadows formed, then two figures stepped out. The first man looked young, but appearances, in his case, were greatly deceiving. Mael had heard many stories about Triarius. The mask covering half the man's face sparkled in the light.

"Good evening. I am Triarius, Brandon. My Son Aldrich was your Father."

"Was?" Brandon stood and turned around to face Triarius. For a moment, he seemed shocked into silence. Most were upon meeting Triarius, though Mael had the feeling, for the younger generations anyway, it was the mask and not the reputation. "What do you mean?"

The man behind Triarius rested a hand on his shoulder and squeezed. Triarius sighed. "I had no choice but to destroy him."

Mael watched the proceedings silently. He knew Cornelius likely understood the ramifications even if Brandon didn't. They were all walking a very fine razor's edge with allowing Diocourides to absorb the Brotherhood into the Romanorum. He had yet to question the eldest on that, though he wanted to do so. As if reading his thoughts, Dio glanced over at him. Mael simply shook his head in answer.

"I swear to you," Triarius said, his attention on Brandon and no one else. "I will not ask you to leave. I relinquish all rights." To Cornelius, he said, "Please, take care of him."

"Thank you. I could never live without Cornelius."

Triarius smiled and slipped his arm around his companion. "As I could never live without Lance and Apollonius. You are happy here, Brandon, and I wish you and Cornelius nothing but the best."

"They are joining me in Rome," Dio said with a warm smile. "Should you ever wish to visit, you are more than welcome, Brandon. You as well, Cornelius."

"I suppose sooner or later I could spare my magician for a short time since Brandon won't go anywhere without him." Knowing unless he made the same invitation, Triarius would have to petition to visit, Mael added, "I also welcome you into my court should you wish to see Brandon, Triarius."

Triarius bowed his head. "Thank you." He extended a hand to Brandon. "We must be leaving. Thank you, all of you, for allowing me this chance." He shook Brandon's hand, then offered his hand to Cornelius. The mage nodded before shaking it.

Dio stood, joining Triarius and his companion. Before they left, he turned to Mael. "I will return tomorrow evening, Mael. We have some matters to discuss."

"The same time will be fine, Diocourides."

Cornelius whispered to Brandon, "We should talk in private as well."

Brandon took Cornelius' hand. "Um... we'll, uh... we'll be in our room." With that, he practically dragged the mage out.

When they were gone, Cian got up and started pacing incessantly. "What the hell is going on?"

"Concerning what?" Mael remained relaxed in his seat; though he knew Cian would have more questions than he could probably answer.

"Everything." Cian shuddered, his agitation growing.

Mael stood and went to him. Strong arms circled the angel's waist and drew him backward. "It might help if you calm down and talk to me."

"He's a rogue, Mael. Triarius is a rogue. It's in my nature to destroy them, and yet, I can't. Why did Diocourides pardon them?"

He gently turned Cian to look at him. "I understand some of the reasoning for what Diocourides is doing, yet some of it eludes me. He pardoned them because they can still function within our world and by our laws. Diocourides wouldn't put the Romanorum at risk if he had any doubts."

Cian sighed, head resting on Mael's shoulder. "What happened with the Brotherhood? What made Triarius change?"

"I'm not sure, but I understand it's been clear for some time the majority of them wanted to be reintegrated into our society." Mael smoothed his hand over Cian's golden hair. "I am also a rogue by your strict definition, love. Like Triarius, I haven't killed a mortal in centuries, yet there was a time when I did."

"I know," Cian murmured. "I've always known that about you." He lifted his head and looked at Mael. "I assume we will have some new people show up to live here?"

"That we will, but I will be keeping a very close eye on them. None of us can afford any problems. It will be a headache, but we'll manage like we always do." Mael gave his angel a wry smile. "I also know it will be rough on you, but I'm asking you not to attack any of the Inferi unless they do something that warrants it."

Cian rolled his eyes and chuckled. "Yes, your Excellency."

* * *

Safe in their room, Brandon dropped down onto the bed, his expression one of pure shell-shock. "What just happened?"

"Your life has changed a great deal." Cornelius sat beside his lover, giving Brandon a sympathetic look. "Things will be the same, yet they will be different."

Brandon blinked. "I don't even know what it all means. I've been so happy here, focusing on magic and us, and now... this?"

"Your status has most definitely changed. You're no longer an anonymous rogue. That's a good thing, as is the protection of Diocourides and his family." Cornelius wrapped an arm around Brandon, then stretched out on his back, drawing his young lover with him.

Brandon rested his head on Cornelius' shoulder. "I don't want it," he said quietly. "All I want is you."

"You have me. Nobody can take you from my side. Not anymore." With a slight turn of his head, he met Brandon's gaze. "But it's not that simple. You have no clue of what being a first formula means, what kind of future is out there for you. You're not going to be able to make any kind of decision until you do."

"What does it mean to be first formula?"

"For starters, it means a great many people will be interested in you. It means, one day, you could rule a country for the Romanorum, just as Selena once did. You could some day be in a position to help a great many of our kind. I assume Triarius has plans for an official pronouncement. If not, I'd ask Mael to insist on it."

For a moment, Brandon looked as if he'd be sick. "A country? Cornelius, the only time I even want to leave the workroom is when I drag you to bed!"

"It's something you would be trained for." Corny pinched Brandon's cheek and laughed. "By the time you'd have your own country, you'd be well prepared for it. It won't happen tomorrow."

Brandon groaned. "Does it have to happen at all? Will I have to leave now? I can't do that again. Being separated from you the first time nearly killed me."

"I image you can study here as well as any other place, so I wouldn't worry about it." Cornelius frowned, which was a rarity for him these days. "Brandon, I don't want you to dismiss your heritage out of hand without even knowing a thing about it. If I were selfish enough to allow it, I would hope Mael or Diocourides would yank me up short." The frown lightened as he stroked the side of Brandon's face in a tender touch. "We're not going to be separated. Not again. That is the one thing both Triarius and Diocourides agreed to."

Brandon's expression eased and he let out a slow breath. "Okay." He turned his head and kissed Cornelius' hand. "As long as I have you by my side."

"Believe me I know what I'll face when word gets out." A slight nudge of his hand turned Brandon's face to his, and he dropped a soft kiss on Brandon's lips. "I won't let you go. It's just not an option. No matter what any of them think. You'll need to be prepared, though. Quite a few will protest someone of my lower status being your father. While I have power and a considerable position here, I won't be considered worthy of you."

"Lower status? What do you mean?"

"I am a second formula. My line isn't as prestigious as yours. I can hold my own among other second formulas, but firsts are out of my league. Under normal circumstances, you would be taught by a first formula."

"Out of your league?" Brandon laughed. "Babe, have you looked in a mirror lately? Do you have any idea how utterly spellbinding you are?"

The comment earned a raised brow, and he answered tongue-in-cheek. "I realize I am far more gorgeous than the others, but that's not what counts in the upper stratosphere, young man."

Brandon rolled them until he straddled Cornelius. He sat up and ran his hands down Cornelius' chest. "Who cares what the rest of them think? Can't please everybody, and besides, the only person I want to please is you."

"I know, and I feel the same. Nobody else worries me except for the headache they will cause us." Hands on Brandon's hips, Cornelius grinned up at him. "By the way, aren't we supposed to be in the workroom?"

"Technically, yes." Brandon rocked his hips a little. "This is more comfortable, I have to admit."

"Teasing will get you everything you want." In one swift movement, Cornelius had Brandon's shirt off. A light pinch to Brandon's nipples followed.

Brandon hissed, hands fisting in the material of Cornelius' robe. "Promise?"

Cornelius chuckled and ground his hips upward. "It's a promise once your clothes are off."

Brandon scrambled up and stripped off his jeans. Then he sprawled on his back. With a wicked grin, he crooked a finger, beckoning Cornelius to him. "Your turn."

Cornelius took his time unbuttoning his robe, perfectly content to revel in the sight of his young lover, spread out for him like a banquet. Clothing gone, he nudged Brandon's thighs open and bent for a kiss. Brandon's legs circled his waist and Cornelius put up no resistance as Brandon tugged him down.

Warm skin beneath his hands and lips, Cornelius licked his way along Brandon's jaw, down his neck. He wanted so badly to drink, but if he did, he knew he'd never stop until they both came. And he wanted it last.

"Cornelius..."

He braced himself on one arm and nuzzled Brandon's throat, while the other hand closed around his lover's flesh. Brandon moaned and thrust, the slide of hardened silk wearing down Cornelius' resolve to take it slow tonight.

"Please," Brandon whispered, entire body beginning to writhe sensually.

To hell with waiting.

Cornelius surged back up for another kiss. He released Brandon and somehow found the lube on the table by the bed. With a final lick to kiss-swollen lips, he sat up and slicked himself. Brandon's gaze fastened on his hand, and Cornelius felt the stare like a touch. He braced himself once more on his other arm, lined up, and pushed in deep.

"Yes..." Brandon groaned, eyes rolling, hips lifting to meet Cornelius.

"So exquisite," Cornelius murmured. Nothing in this world compared to the sight before him. He kept the strokes deep and slow, not wanting to miss a single expression.

Then those eyes opened and he was lost.

Need took over everything else and Cornelius kissed his lover hard. It took only a few thrusts, a few rocks of Brandon's hips into him, and Cornelius had no chance of stopping. Nudging Brandon's head to the side, he sank his fangs into Brandon's throat.

Brandon shouted and bucked beneath him. Sweetened blood flowed over Cornelius' tongue as Brandon's body convulsed around his length. Heat spread between them, and Cornelius followed, barely licking the wounds before his own release washed over him.

After a few moments of recuperation, he eased out. Brandon cleaned them both, then smiled before snuggling close. Cornelius held tight, refusing to let even the truth of Brandon's heritage intrude on the contentment. They'd deal with the rest later. Much later.

Chapter Two

"Dio?" Josh's voice rose above the drone of the court secretary and captured Dio's attention. He approached close enough to whisper in Dio's ear. "There's something weird in the bedroom mirror. You might want to see it."

One brow rose, but Dio knew his companion wouldn't disturb him unless necessary. A wave of his hand silenced the litany from his secretary. "Later, Roberto."

Roberto bowed and left the office, shutting the door behind him. Josh returned his attention to Dio. "I wouldn't have bothered you, but... well, just come with me." He went through the door to their bedroom and, once inside, gestured toward the tall, free-standing mirror in a corner.

Intrigued more than alarmed, Dio followed without comment. He slid an arm around Josh's waist as he paused in front of the mirror. At first, there appeared to be no more than a blurry outline of something possibly human in shape, then a black liquid filled the outer edges of the image.

"Demonic. Highly unusual."

Smoke emanated from the frame, and the image became the clear shape of a raven-haired man with an amused expression. "Very impressive, Diocourides. You know the powers."

The laughter in the demon's voice drew a smile from Dio. "And you are?"

"The name is Sagan. I thought this would be the best, most non-threatening way to contact you. Don't wish to impose and all that, but needs do drive a devil. May I come before you? No harm intended or given."

Josh tensed. "Dio, is this really a good idea?"

"I've heard of you. It seems what I was told of your odd nature is true." Dio studied the handsome features of the demon in silence before he made his decision. "No harm to any in this room and you may enter." He turned to Josh with a smile. "It is never a good idea to deal with most demons, but there are a few exceptions. However, if I ever catch you doing anything like this without me, you will pay dearly, young man."

"No chance of that happening," Josh muttered. He backed up a bit, putting distance between himself and the figure stepping through the mirror. The demon stretched as if waking from a long nap.

"I have no intention of harming anyone," Sagan said. "What I do have, however, is a warning."

Dio remained cordial, though a bit wary. "A warning of... ?"

"All I can tell you is there are several people you need near you. Something is stirring over the horizon, something considerably stronger than I like."

"Something stronger than Dio?" Josh asked.

Sagan regarded Josh with the slightest hint of amusement. "There are many in existence—and beyond it—who are more powerful than Diocourides."

"No other hint, Sagan?"

"You know as well as I do, old man: I'm limited in what I can give away. You need an angel, that much is certain. A prince might be a good idea, too, for when things get... hairy. It's about all I can do for you. Any more and it puts the old creation/

space-time continuum out of whack. The rest you have to figure out."

"That does narrow the field somewhat. I do appreciate the warning. If there's ever anything else you can reveal-"

"You'll be the first to know. I'm not about to approach through normal channels, though. Not a good idea for either of us."

When the demon vanished the way he'd entered, Josh turned to Dio. "A prince and an angel? Mael and Cian?"

"They would be the only angel and prince I know. Most unusual for a demon to carry a warning, even one as different as Sagan." He eyed Josh, lost in thought, unsure of how much he should try to hide. It would require little effort on Dio's part to conceal his real concern over the vague warning, but it wasn't his habit to keep things from Josh.

"What's wrong? I know that look."

"Sagan is right. There are a number of creatures more powerful than I am. Not many, but they do exist. Just the fact a demon came to warn me signals how much trouble I can expect. It's not good. Not good at all. It wouldn't be wise to let others know anything until we learn more ourselves."

"What do we do?" Josh asked. "Do you really think Mael and Cian will leave London and come here?"

"If I need him, Mael will do as I ask. I'm not sure about the angel, but I believe he will follow Mael wherever he has to. The only way to get Mael here, without raising suspicion, is to offer him a place in the Inner Circle." After he settled at the edge of the bed, he reached for Josh. "It's something I planned on doing, just not so soon. The man has proven his worth several times over, and no one will be surprised by my choice."

Josh joined him on the bed, legs draped over Dio's. "Who would take over London if they left?"

"It's a pity his boy Christian hasn't had any experience as yet. It's time to put him in a position to eventually take over for his Father. I can't trust that damn Nigel to help, but I've no doubt Mael's second can make do during the necessary absence."

"Cornelius is going to just love that," Josh laughed. "It'll mean leaving his workroom."

"For the time being, it will have to do. London has always been secure enough to weather just about anything. The British are remarkable creatures in that respect." Dio reached out, hand gentle against Josh's cheek. "If it becomes bad enough, I will have to send you away. I'm wondering if I should do it anyway."

Josh turned his face and kissed Dio's palm. "Please don't," he whispered. "Not yet. If things turn sour, I'll go without argument, I promise."

"I'll hold you to your word the minute it becomes necessary. For the time being, things will remain as always."

Josh smiled. "Thank you. Leaving will be hard enough, even if it's only temporary. Don't blame me for wanting to stall as long as possible."

* * *

Firelight danced off gold, brilliant sparkles reflecting on the ceiling and walls in an otherwise dim room. A breastplate bearing a flaming sword lay over a pillow. Greaves and gauntlets rested beside it. The rest of the armor spread out on the bed in various states of polishing.

Cian knelt before the stone altar in his tower. Despite living in the palace, he came here to pray. Only two others knew where to find him and how to get here. His head bowed, he kept his eyes closed, hands on his naked thighs, palms upward. Something drove him here, a disquiet he couldn't pinpoint. Yet no matter how much he meditated, answers eluded him.

"What am I missing?" he whispered. "It's just beyond my reach."

A presence he knew like his own soul filled the room and Cian sighed as he stood. "Don't worry about disturbing me. I can't focus anyway." He moved the armor off the bed, given Mael's rather deadly allergy to gold, and gestured his prince over.

"I take it something is bothering you, as well." Mael joined him beside the bed. "I had been enjoying an abnormally peaceful night until an hour ago."

"Dare I ask?"

"I was hoping you'd tell me what is bothering you first."

"I honestly wish I could explain it," Cian said. "Something stirs, something dark. But no amount of contemplation is helping." He lay down and pulled the prince onto the bed with him. At least in Mael's arms, the turmoil lessened—for the time being, anyway. "Even Michael can't put a name to it."

"When you did talk to Michael?" Mael loosened his tie, pulled it away from his neck, and dropped it nearby.

"Who do think I pray to? Your turn."

"I've been summoned to Rome, and also told to ask you to tell Michael that Selena would be needed. It's not unusual for Dio to request my presence, but Selena is something else. It makes me think your feeling is dead on." The former first formula ruler of the UK and Mael's ex-nemesis, Selena, was no longer an official part of the Romanorum. For all intents and purposes, she was dead on earth since she resided in Heaven alongside Michael.

Cian sat up, half-leaning over Mael, propped on one arm. "Rome? Did Dio say anything else? If anyone else has sensed something brewing, I imagine it would be him."

"No, it was just a request to see us both. Whatever is going on, Dio doesn't want any hint to leak out. The request for Selena wasn't even part of his official invitation. Something is wrong. No doubt about that."

"I'd be lying if I said I didn't think Dio's summons and my concerns were related," Cian said, absently tracing a fingertip along the front of Mael's shirt. "This isn't a trivial issue. Something—or someone—is waking."

"Well, there's not much we can do until we speak to Dio. He wants us in his office tonight." Mael captured Cian's hand and brought it to his mouth.

Tracing the contours of Mael's lips with his fingertip, Cian bit back a groan. "Not one for advanced notice, is he?"

"The father of all vampires really doesn't have to worry about things like that."

Cian rolled his eyes. "Well, I haven't been to Rome in quite a while. Should be interesting, to say the least."

"The political intrigue is even worse than in my court. I spent more than a few centuries thriving in the atmosphere.

Cian traced a line down Mael's chin, over his throat. "Aside from all of this, what else is on your mind?"

"Like you, I'm not entirely certain. I've received a few reports of unusual activity among weres. We've had an odd influx during the last week. My court is having hissy fits every time I turn around. Tensions are already rising without whatever Dio is hiding."

"Lee said something about that today. He's been working alongside Sav to keep an eye on things. We both thought it might be some of Aldrich's followers still lurking about, but apparently there's just as much tension on the were side as there is here. So far, nothing noteworthy has happened, but Lee feels energy fluctuations like I do. You think they might be connected—the were troubles and whatever's going on in Rome?"

"I'm trying not to make too many assumptions until I talk to Dio." The prince tugged Cian down for a light kiss. "I think your little vacation might be at an end for the time being."

Cian chuckled softly. "You talk like I've been in the tower for days. It's only been a few hours." He threaded his fingers through Mael's hair.

"Time has a tendency to drag, my angel. Or have you never noticed?"

Cian nipped his lover's bottom lip. "I'm over three thousand years old, Mael. Time means little."

"As much as I would love to do nothing more than remain here for the evening, we had better get to Rome."

With a sigh, Cian got up. As soon as he dressed, Mael gathered him close. Just like his own portals that allowed him travel anywhere, Mael's shadows were incredibly convenient. The 'trip' took only a few moments.

Upon their arrival, they were escorted through the quiet marble halls of the Romanorum. Graceful, white arches rose high above their heads. Ancient reliefs carved into the walls fit well with the modern crystal chandeliers sparkling from the ceiling. The man escorting them to Dio's office gestured toward a closed door, bowed deeply to Mael and Cian, and waited for them to enter.

"Thank you, Roberto." Mael opened the door and followed Cian inside.

Dio sat at his desk, game controller in hand and fingers furious on the buttons. From the couch, Josh called out encouragement. Cian just shook his head. Diocourides never ceased to amaze him. The man, despite being thousands of years old, acted like a teenager at times. On a large TV screen, a soldier scurried around a corner of a building and others hurried past him.

"Dammit, you guys suck. Somebody cover me here, will you?"

Other voices filled the room from the game, yelling commands as Dio continued to guide his character on the screen amidst what sounded like machine gun fire.

"Out of my way, asswipe." When Dio's character darted to the right, another character behind him took the bullet instead.

Dio utterly a litany of foul curses and Josh laughed. "Are you sure you don't suck, too?"

"Hush, brat. Oh, hey, guys," Dio said, eyes fixed on the screen. "Give me a minute here. With these idiots, I'm about to die anyway."

Sure enough, not more than a few seconds later, the image on the screen wavered and a red haze filled it. With a growl, Dio tossed the controller on his desk. "I'm out, guys."

Master of protocol, Mael bowed reverently. "It is my honor to serve in whatever capacity you need, Diocourides."

"Oh, do sit, Mael, and remove the glass rod from your ass while you're at it."

Cian chuckled and pushed Mael into the nearest chair before dropping down onto the prince's lap. "Lee loves that game. You two would thoroughly enjoy trashing one another."

"Is he any good?" An interested gleam shone in Dio's eyes.

"I think he is, but I'm not exactly a good judge of games." Cian shifted until he got comfortable, Mael's arms going around his waist. "He's at court a lot these days, ever since he fell in love with Mael's assassin."

"Give me his online name later. For now, we've got more serious things to discuss." Josh wandered over to Dio's side and settled on the arm of his chair. Dio flashed him a quick smile before he returned his attention to Mael and Cian.

"Cian will speak to Michael and Selena as soon as possible. Now what is all of this about?" Mael asked.

"I've been given an unexpected warning. A demon by the name of Sagan approached me and told me something is going on from a very powerful direction. He could give no real details, other than I needed you two."

Cian glanced down at Mael, then back to Dio. "Then it isn't just me. Michael and I both have noticed a... shift in balance. We can't pinpoint where it's coming from, though. Something is going on—something infinitely dark."

"Sagan said it was something stronger than me," Dio said.

"There are few possibilities among the Fae" Mael added, "but none I know of would choose to interfere in the human realm. The punishment isn't worth it."

"It's... old," Cian said. "Much older than anything we've all experienced, and much stronger than Fae."

"No vampire would qualify since I am the most powerful. No were tribe has any real kind of power. The spirit realm isn't a possibility either. There might be a wizard or two; however, they rarely leave their own realm. It might be a demon, but that is nothing Lucifer can't handle. Nor would Sagan have come to me if it were. That leaves something we probably know nothing of. For the first time in my existence, I am puzzled."

"It would be in your best interest if I remain in Rome," Mael said.

"I won't argue there," Cian said. "We'll need someone to hold down the fort while we're gone. The one person I know of isn't going to like the idea."

"I already have things in motion, but for now, I will ask for Selena's help on that. London is one of our most stable cities even with its problems. Between her and your second, London will remain safe. My word will be enough to insure it. In order to avoid questions and suspicion, I will announce Mael's acceptance of my offer of a position in the Inner Circle. Everyone here believes that is why I called you to Rome."

"And what of my Father? Nigel will be beside himself at the promotion."

"Leave him to me, Mael," Dio said. "He won't interfere, and you will stay here in the Romanorum with me."

"Good luck containing him."

Cian rested back against Mael. "You weren't kidding when you said Inner Circle politics made London a walk in the park, were you, *cariad*?"

"You don't know the half of it," Mael muttered.

Dio motioned Josh off his chair and stood. "I expect you to return to Rome in a few days and settle in here. You'll be given quarters in my wing as a 'thank you' from me. It makes a nice retreat from the others since none dare bother me there. Only Roberto is allowed." He held his hand out to Cian. "I do appreciate your willingness to go along with this, Cian. I know it's a weird request."

"Where Mael goes, I go," Cian said as he shook Dio's hand. "After what we've been through, I don't think either of us is willing to let the other out of sight."

"It doesn't matter what you need, you know you have it from me." Mael shook Dio's hand when it was offered, then released it to take Cian's. After he bowed once again to Dio, he pulled Cian with him out of the office.

"What are your thoughts?" Cian asked once he and Mael were alone in the hall.

"Far more troubled than I like."

Shadows enveloped them and the world disappeared into the blackness for a long moment. When the shadows faded, they stood in their bedroom in the London palace. Cian locked the door and smiled. He stood before Mael and rubbed the prince's shoulders in an effort to ease the tense muscles.

"So let me settle them."

"We have very little time before I need to drag Cornelius into this and prepare everyone for the advent of Selena." Mael slipped his hand beneath the edge of Cian's shirt to disrobe him. "I'll gladly steal what I can get."

Cian caught Mael's tie and lured him in for a kiss. "How do you want me, my prince?"

Mael licked his angel's lips and worked Cian's pants open. Fingers catching the waistband, he sank to his knees, kissing the warm skin beneath his lips. "Any way I can have you."

When he reached Cian's cock, he drew it into his mouth, suckling on the tip. Cian hissed and fisted both hands in Mael's hair. He let Cian stroke in and out a few times before he pulled back and stood. Taking his angel's hand, he lured Cian to the bed. Mael stripped off the last of his clothing and lay on his back. A moment later, Cian straddled him, both of them groaning at the contact.

"Ride me." Mael stretched enough to reach the lube and slicked two fingers. Then he slipped them under Cian and eased them into blessedly tight heat.

"Mael..." Cian's eyes drifted shut and he began rocking. "In me. Please."

Unable to ignore such a request, Mael replaced his fingers with his cock. He arched as Cian's body closed around him. The movements were unhurried, Cian rising and falling with every stroke Mael made. With one hand braced on the bed by Mael's head, Cian leaned down and kissed him. Mael felt the angel's other hand pumping himself in time to the thrusts.

"Mael." Cian sped up his hand and hips, his breathing growing shallow.

Refusing to let his lover come without tasting, Mael rolled them. He struck swift and deep, and Cian tensed a split second before his angel shouted. Heat spilled between them and he followed. He growled against Cian's throat, the sweet, arousal-laced blood only adding to the fuel that sent him over the edge.

It took several moments before either of them could move, much less speak. Mael eased out and lay on his back, drawing Cian to him. He had no idea what to expect once they got to Rome, but he thanked every god in existence that he didn't have to face it alone.

Chapter Three

"You rang, boss?"

Mael had already put off warning Cornelius for an entire night and day. It couldn't be avoided any longer. Deciding not to beat around the bush, he said, "Cian and I have to go to Rome soon. For how long, I'm not sure. I need you to play first in command until we return."

"Are you kidding?" Cornelius plopped into the chair in front of Mael's desk. He might bitch, but he was already resigned to it. "You know how I hate being dragged out of my workroom, Mael."

"I know you do, but since Diocourides wants us in Rome, you're stuck." Mael knew the decision wouldn't be popular with his magician. He wasn't above a bit of bribery. "I'll pay your bill with M and G for a year."

Cornelius brightened a bit, then shook his head. "You know I'll do it anyway. You can give me an early birthday gift if you're feeling generous, though."

Mael laughed. "Done. And Happy Birthday."

"So what's so important for you to high tail it to Rome? Is this official or unofficial?"

"Unofficial because Diocourides received a warning from a demon. Official as in I'm being offered a temporary position in the Inner Circle, although no one knows it's temporary."

"Oh, one of those. A demon you say? How strange." Cornelius peered at Mael over the edge of his spectacles before he helped himself to the bottle of brandy on Mael's desk.

"Unusual for a being like that to stir himself over vampire matters."

"The warning was too cryptic to be of much use, other than Cian and I will be needed in Rome." Mael took the glass the mage offered him.

"Do be careful, Mael. I'd hate for anything to happen to you."

"I'd hate it, too."

The remark earned him the mage's trademark 'oh, how witty' look. "This really is a bad time. I'm in the middle of working with your and Cian's blood. It's a delicate process to add two bloods to the formula, you know. Did Diocourides say when he'd return?"

"No, but I'm sure it won't be much longer. He's as eager as you to perfect this."

Cornelius finished off his brandy, set the glass down, and stood. "Speaking of which, I can't leave my potions alone for long. Two of them are close to critical stage."

"If we're still in Rome once it's done, I'll make arrangements to use it there."

"Has Cian chosen yet?"

"He has somebody in mind."

An air of excitement replaced the earlier morose mood. "I am looking forward to this. So hard to wait for its first use." On his way out the door, the mage continued muttering to himself. "It will take at least another two weeks. But maybe if I..."

The door shut, cutting off the rambling. Mael drained his brandy and stood. That had gone better than he'd expected. Cornelius had the skills and power necessary to run London all on his own; the man just didn't want to.

Shadows gathered at Mael's command, and he stepped through them into his private quarters. For the most part, it had been a quiet night, and he had a few hours to relax until he needed to attend his court session. Once he'd stripped and dressed for comfort in his favorite black velvet robe, Mael poured another glass of brandy. A fire crackled in the bedroom fireplace along with the sound of one of Mael's favorite songs in the background. Book in one hand and glass in the other, he settled in one of the comfortable chair to relax.

"Am I imagining things," Cian said as he walked into the room, closing the door behind him, "or do we really have a moment's peace to just relax and talk?" He pulled off his shirt, and, for the first time in a long while, let his wings unfurl and stretch.

"Things are settled for the time being, and I'm taking full advantage before the chaos hits. Care to join me?" Mael waved his glass in an airy fashion.

Cian smiled and poured himself some wine before getting comfortable at Mael's feet. "I saw him again."

He knew little about the mortal Cian had been watching. Though Mael had yet to met the boy, he had no objections to Cian's desire for a son. "And when are you planning on speaking to him? Or have you already?"

"Tonight." Cian took a sip of his wine and stared into the fire, the light of the flames turning his golden hair an otherworldly shade of red. "If I don't do something, he'll die on the streets. It's December, and the clothing he wears is threadbare at best."

"Have you decided it's to be him?" Mael rested his hand on Cian's head, fingers toying with the gold strands. "If you have, it's time to bring him here."

"I have no doubt in my soul he's the one." Cian sighed. "I've watched him for a while now. Every time he sells his body to survive, he loses another part of himself."

"Tell me more about him. You've really said little since we first discussed this." He'd left the decision up to Cian, more than happy to accept the angel's choice in the matter. However, he sensed Cian was close to bringing the boy to the palace, so it was time he learned more.

"Taylor is twenty-two. According to people who know him, he's been on the streets since he was sixteen. He's gay, which I imagine has a good bit to do with why his parents kicked him out. Though some say it's also because he's pagan." Cian fell silent for a moment before continuing. "There's something about him. When I'm around, observing him, I don't make my presence known. Yet... it's as if he senses I'm there."

"Cornelius knew what you were, and so did Brandon, but they are exceptional in their abilities. Does this one have magical ability as well?"

"I think he might have an aptitude for it, but this is different. This isn't so much magic as it is... intuition, I think." Cian shook his head. "Whatever it is, it's what drew me to him so strongly."

"I believe you've made a wise choice. I trust your instincts as well as I trust my own, Cian. I'll arrange for a suite of rooms near ours for the boy. I would also suggest you buy what he needs since it doesn't sound as if he has much. Ben should be able to help you with it. It won't be a problem to get what's necessary and in a short amount of time.

"I will." Cian stood and leaned forward, giving Mael a soft kiss. "I need to find him before it gets much colder outside. I love you."

"Take care of what you need to." Mael chuckled. "I will remind you how much you love me many times when you return."

Cian laughed and put his shirt back on. He grabbed his long leather coat off the bed and headed out.

Mael picked up his book once more and immersed himself in its pages. It wasn't hard to lose himself in Shakespeare, and the bell sounded an hour passed before Mael realized the time had gone by. Another knock on his door interrupted any further reading, and Mael set his book aside as he called out, "Come in."

Christian walked in with a grin. "You busy, dad?"

"Just enjoying some Shakespeare before I have to attend court."

Christian didn't move far from the door. "Do you need me there? If not, I'm heading out for the night with Alexander."

"You need to be there tonight, son. Cian will be bringing Taylor home."

"Is that one he picked?" Mild interest flickered in Christian's eyes.

"He's the one, and I'd like to show the boy some friendly faces. You know how intimating this place can be."

"I should say. What's he like? Have you met him?"

"I haven't met him yet, but I trust Cian's instincts. Something draws him to this boy, and that's enough for me."

Christian nodded in agreement. "I better change." He gestured to his casual jeans and shirt. "This won't cut it for a session."

* * *

One foot in front of the other. Ignore the accusing stares. Don't let them in.

Taylor Reed flipped up the collar of his worn denim jacket, shielding his neck from the bitter cold wind. Mid-December. He would be lucky if he survived to the New Year. Most of his friends, if he could call them that, were out of town. No one knew he didn't have a place anyway. Maybe it was his pride talking, but he wasn't the type to beg. He stopped walking and stared up at the building looming before him. He hated coming here, but when the alternative was freezing to death on a park bench, he figured selling his body for a few hours on a dirty mattress wasn't such a big deal.

Just as he put a hand on the door, he caught a glimpse of someone in the glass. The man stood tall, well-built, with long, curly blond hair. His steady gaze held Taylor immobile, unable to open the door.

"You don't have to do it."

"What?" Taylor turned and met those unnatural blue eyes head-on.

The man nodded at the door. "Sell yourself."

Taylor bristled and started to walk away. "Fuck you."

"I'm sorry." The man walked evenly with him.

Stopping abruptly, Taylor glared at him. "Why is an angel out in the middle of the street at night, anyway?"

"How do you know?"

Taylor shrugged and crossed his arms, rubbing them to keep the circulation going under the bite of a harsh wind. "I just do. Gut feeling."

"Please, let me help you."

"Why? Who are you and why would you care?"

The man slipped off his leather coat and draped it around Taylor's shoulders. It was heavy and smelled herbal. A hint of the man's personal scent mingled with a touch of old leather. "Because I do."

Sighing, Taylor nodded.

"Are you hungry?"

"Yeah," Taylor admitted, though he wasn't about to say when the last time he'd eaten. Hell, he wasn't sure himself. "What's your name?"

"Cian Carmichael."

Why did that name sound familiar? Taylor knew that name, though he had no idea why. Maybe he'd heard it somewhere. The man looked well off. Taylor held out a hand, trying to still it from shaking in the cold. "Taylor Reed."

"Come on," Cian said. He shook Taylor's hand, then put an arm around Taylor's shoulders. "Let's find some place warm."

Taylor stiffened a little, but he let Cian lead him down the sidewalk. They found a small diner still open and went inside. Taylor followed Cian to a booth near the back and slid into the opposite seat. A bored-looking waitress came over and handed them two menus.

"What can I get you to drink?" she asked, flipping out a notepad.

"Guinness," Cian said.

When the waitress wandered off, Cian sat back in his seat and Taylor found himself the subject of an intense but curious gaze. He'd been under scrutiny before, usually at the mercy of a man hard up for a good fuck. Cian was different, though. Despite the whole angel thing, which Taylor still wasn't sure how he knew, Cian wasn't like anyone else. Then it hit Taylor like a ton of bricks.

"Holy shit. You're with the vampires here."

Cian smiled and nodded once. "I'm Mael Black's companion."

Oh, God.

Taylor swallowed, grateful for the break in conversation when the waitress arrived with their drinks. They both gave their orders, then she left again. Taylor stared into the dark liquid in his glass, trying to work out how he managed to garner the attention of the vampire prince's consort.

"You have nothing to fear, if that's your concern."

"Then why are you here?" Taylor asked, sipping on his drink to keep the bombardment of questions down. He'd slept with vampires before, but he'd never asked about court life, even though he wanted to know what it was like. Hell, he'd never even been bitten.

"I've been watching you, Taylor. I know how you live, how you survive on the streets when most would've died—either by their hand or another's. I know what you do for a place to stay and food to eat."

Taylor wanted to sink into the floor under the table. Here was this powerful man, partnered with an even more powerful man, and Taylor felt transparent. "I..."

"Listen to me." Cian leaned forward and the warmth of his hand seeped through Taylor's chilled skin, heating his fingers faster than any fire. "I want to help you, Taylor. Please let me."

"How?"

"Come back to the palace with me."

Eyes wide, Taylor couldn't believe what he just heard. "What? Why me?"

"Because..." Cian seemed to think on something for a moment. "Because I care. You could have a new life, one in which you'd never have to worry or want for anything ever again."

"Would I become a vampire?"

Cian glanced down at their hands, his still clasping Taylor's. "Yes, though you'd share my blood along with the prince's."

This was just... Taylor tried sorting everything out in his head and nothing made sense. Why him? Why not someone better? "Why do you want me, instead of someone else?"

"I want a son, Taylor. I've watched you for several months and I know you're the one I want. You don't have to give me an answer now. I only wanted to tell you, to give you time to think it over."

Everything Taylor had ever wanted—a home, a family, a life off the streets and out of strange beds—sat before him on a silver platter. So why the hell couldn't he bring himself to say yes?

* * *

An hour and a half later, Taylor stood staring up at a mansion. Not just any mansion, either. This one just happened to be the home of Prince Mael Black. Beside him, Cian nodded to the guard at the gate and they were granted entrance. When the front door opened for them, Taylor stepped inside behind Cian... and immediately felt like the proverbial fish out of water.

"Oh, my God..."

The foyer was bigger than any place he'd ever seen. A staircase led up one flight, and hallways lined either side, on both floors. Voices drifted from every direction. Taylor swallowed. What the hell was he doing here?

"Come on," Cian said. "I'd like you to meet Mael."

"The... the prince?"

Cian chuckled. "The one and only, and believe me, that's a good thing at times."

One of the servants bowed to Cian before he stepped forward to open the throne room doors for them.

"More reports are coming in, your Excellency." A young woman, clad in black, stood before a throne on a dais. There were two men on the dais, and Taylor assumed the man on the throne had to be the prince. Another man, eerily similar to the prince, stood beside him.

Cian waited until the woman finished speaking and the prince glanced away from her. With a smile, Cian headed for the dais. Taylor followed him, completely dumbstruck. When they reached the dais, Cian bowed, though Taylor thought he saw the angel give the prince a wink.

The young man beside the prince flashed Cian a smile before he addressed Mael. "I can help Sav, Father. I know a bit about weres from my time in America. His Eminence, Nikolai, took an odd notion to allow them on his estate."

"If Sav is agreeable, that's fine, Christian."

"Certainly, your Excellency. I would appreciate his help."

"That's enough for now, Sav."

She bowed to him as Mael focused back on Cian. "You're back early."

Cian stepped to the side and afforded Taylor his first full look at London's vampire prince. "I told you I would find him." He motioned for Taylor to come closer. "Prince Black, this is Taylor Reed. Taylor, this is the illustrious—and occasionally infuriating—Prince Mael Black."

Eyes wide, Taylor froze for a moment. Then he figured he'd do what Cian had done. He bowed, albeit awkwardly. "Hi..."

"The bowing is only necessary when court is in session," the prince chuckled. "Cian does it for his own amusement." A wry smile curved Mael's lips. He stood and descended the few steps to join them. The young man followed behind him.

"Hello, Taylor. Welcome to my court. This is my son, Christian." A warm smile softened the darker edge of the prince's features.

"Thank you," Taylor said. The prince's smile went a long way to easing him.

"Father told me you'd be joining us." Christian offered a friendly smile as well.

When he turned to the prince's son, however, Taylor found himself at a loss for words for a moment. Christian looked like Mael, but younger, and a bit more lithe. Not to mention, the man was drop-dead gorgeous.

Finally remembering he had a brain, Taylor nodded. "Nice to meet you, too."

"I look forward to getting to know you better, Taylor," Mael said. "Don't let everything overwhelm you. For the time being, you can settle in and not worry too much about the court itself."

"I'll be more than happy to show him around and get him settled in, Father," Christian said.

"You do that..." Cian muttered, attention thoroughly distracted, it seemed, as the prince tugged him close for a kiss.

Taylor blinked at the unabashed display, then looked to Christian. "Are they always like that?"

"Worse." Christian grinned. "You'll get used to them."

"Not used to seeing it so... openly," Taylor said.

"They'll come back to Earth, sooner or later. Come on. I'll take you to your quarters. At least with you around, it makes a good excuse to avoid the sycophants." The door opened for them then closed behind them as Christian led the way up the wide staircase. "Take notes so you don't get lost."

"No kidding." Taylor followed Christian, only slightly trying not to watch the man walk. Damn. "So, uh... are you Mael's vampire son?"

Christian flashed fang at him. "I really shouldn't do that. It's not polite, but I can't resist. Yes, I am. I've heard you're up for the position as well."

Purposely ignoring how hot the vampire looked, Taylor focused on the conversation. "That's the rumor, anyway. How old are you? You don't look any older than me, and I'm twenty-two."

"I was younger than you by three years. In vampire terms, though, I'm about ninety. Give or take a few years." Christian's gaze ran over Taylor when they stopped in front of one of the doors. "Good thing Cian bought you a few new things. Looks like you need 'em."

"He did?" Taylor looked down and grimaced. "Yeah... I, uh... guess I do."

"Were you homeless or something?" Christian opened the door and waited for Taylor to go inside, then followed him. "Or maybe I shouldn't ask that. Mael didn't say too much about you."

"More or less," Taylor said. "I got by thanks to offering up my..." He trailed off as he got a good look at the room. It dwarfed every other place he'd seen. His gaze, though, settled on the bed and he stood at the end, in quiet disbelief. "It's a bed," he whispered. Not a bench, not a couch, not a dirty mattress riddled with disgusting stains—but a bed. *His* bed.

Christian opened the closet door. "Here's your new stuff. Cian has pretty good taste."

Tearing his gaze from the enormous bed, Taylor peered into the closet. More clothes than he'd ever seen lined the shelves and racks. "How did he..." He shook his head, figuring it was an angel thing. He closed the door.

"You hungry?"

"I could eat a little, yeah."

"Whenever you want anything, all you have to do is tug this." Christian demonstrated with the ornate embroidered bell pull. "A servant will get you what you want. I take it you've had it rougher than I thought. How long were you homeless?"

Taylor sat on the bed and sighed. "Since I was kicked out of my home at sixteen. Parents found out I'm gay and pagan. I've spent the past six years sleeping in parks and hotels whenever I could find someone who'd pay for me."

"Good thing Cian found you. I didn't think you'd been homeless that long." Christian sprawled in one of the recliners, legs dangling over the arm rest. "I'm gay, too, by the way. You'll have it easy here. Worst things you have to put up with are the suck-ups. Being Mael's son brings a hell of a lot of prestige."

A part of Taylor wished Christian hadn't mentioned that bit of information about himself. He didn't think the prince or Cian would take kindly to him being attracted to Christian. "This is all... well, new is an understatement. I'm used to selling my body for what little I could get. This..." He gestured around the room. "How does someone get used to it?"

"It's simpler than you think. You just live here and it becomes normal. You'll be surprised at how easy it is. Except for some of the court. Some vampires can be serious pains in the ass." There was a knock at the door, and Christian called out, "Come on in."

A second later, the door opened and a thin woman in a black uniform dress entered with a large covered tray. A touch of gray in her red hair made her seem older than most Taylor had seen until now. She smiled as she set the tray on a table. "Good evening, Christian, Taylor."

"Hey, Agnes. How's it going tonight?"

"Way too busy as usual." She smiled again before she headed out of the door.

"Selling yourself is something you'll never have to do again. Mael will make sure you're taken care for more centuries than you can think about."

Taylor felt himself blush. "To be honest, Cian is the only one who knew, until now. Unless he told the prince."

"I don't think those two keep anything from each other." Christian stirred to check out what had been brought. "Ah, bless Agnes. She's a sweetheart." Grinning, he picked up a bottle filled with dark red liquid and poured himself a glass. Taylor assumed it was blood. "Help yourself before it gets cold. Hope you like burgers and fries."

"Doesn't everybody?" Taylor laughed. "Speaking of... what's it like, being a vampire?"

Christian appeared quite comfortable, bottle and glass in hand. "Lots of fun, but some of the court protocol can be boring. It's worse in Rome, though, so I shouldn't complain too much. I don't miss food and sun as much as I thought I would. Don't think about it at all unless a mortal is near." He drew a deep breath and laughed. "In fact, you smell even more delicious than an expensive wine."

Taylor nearly choked on the soda that came with his dinner. "What?"

"Believe me, you'll understand when you're a vampire. You'll also make do with bottled blood unless you've a ghoul around to help out. I've never ghouled anyone, so I make do."

"What's a ghoul?"

"A human who drinks vampire blood. They can live as long as a vampire and have some of the powers. They can still go out in sunlight and eat. When you're turned, you'll probably feed from Seth once you're used to it."

"Why haven't you ever had a ghoul?"

"They're a lot of responsibility. And I mean a lot." Something in Christian's expression shuttered. "It's not a wise idea for the foreseeable future."

"Understandable." Taylor started on his food and watched Christian a couple of times when the vampire closed his eyes as he sipped his drink. "How did you end up with the prince?"

Before Christian could answer, the bedroom door opened and Cian stuck his head inside. "Mael is calling a closed court session. He wants you both there."

"Back to work," Christian sighed.

Once Taylor finished his food, they headed back downstairs to the throne room. The woman from before, Sav, waited outside the door. She opened it for them, and they entered together.

Chapter Four

Mael locked the doors with a single thought. Only a certain few were allowed into the meeting concerning the problem with the weres. With everybody present, Mael settled on his throne, his hand casually resting on Cian's. Looking between Ben and Sav, he asked, "Have either of you found out any reasons for what is going on with the were creatures?"

Sav glanced at Ben then back to Mael. "No, your Excellency. For obvious reasons, none of the weres are talking to us. The complaints about their presence are escalating."

"Then tell everyone, unless violence is involved, to stop complaining."

Turning his hand over and lacing his fingers with Mael's, Cian shook his head. "What could possibly be driving weres out of their natural homes and into the city? Have there been any reports of more powerful vampires causing problems beyond the last of Aldrich's people?"

"We've already talked to Diocourides," Ben said. "He's detected no unexplained presences of our kind in any of the areas that don't match Aldrich's men. We've been hunting them down, but they don't seem well organized."

Mael looked over at Cian, tightening his fingers on the angel's hand. "Normally weres prefer areas they can easily hunt in. The city doesn't qualify. Whatever is forcing them out isn't likely to be vampire. Even a vampire such as Diocourides would have problems handling entire tribes of them."

"Do you think there might be trouble from others?" Christian asked. "I've studied enough to know that, although the immediate clans get along with us, there are those on both sides who still harbor a bit of hatred."

"When you have weres and vampires together in any immediate vicinity, both react uneasily." Pinning a quick look on Sav, Mael continued, "Which is why if the complaints don't cease, everybody will find out I'm more to be feared than the damn weres. The immediate concern is to prevent any violence from breaking out. I will insure punishments are harsh on any vampires who start problems."

"If need be, I can call Michael if things get to be too much," Cian said.

"No, I wouldn't want to bother Michael over this. Especially when we have no clue what is happening. Ben, is there any recognizable tribe leader in London?

"Linda Ellsworth. She's put out a call to most of the weres, and they are obeying her orders."

"Good. I want a message sent to her. Tell her to report directly to this court if she encounters problems with any vampires."

"As you wish, your Excellency."

As the others talked amongst themselves for a moment, Cian turned to Mael. "What do you need me to do? I am the only one you have who can go out in daylight for extended periods of time."

Eying his angel in silence, Mael considered a few ideas before he spoke. "Have you ever dealt with any weres?"

"It's been about six hundred years, but yes. What do you need?"

"It might be best if you delivered my message to Linda Ellsworth personally. Try to get her to understand that I have no problems with the weres wanting to remain in London. My interest is in avoiding any trouble between her tribe and my vampires until this is solved."

"I can do that. Anything I need to know?"

"I'm not sure if your word will carry any weight, but it's well known you are my companion. I can always hope she'll listen to you."

"If I can talk a demon into going back to Hell, I can do this. I can even be nice about it."

"Cian will handle Ellsworth, Sav. You continue finding out what you can about the situation."

"Yes, your Excellency."

* * *

The next night Mael ordered another closed session.

"How bad is it getting, Sav?"

"The numbers are increasing, your Excellency. So far, we have several were tribes either holed up in hotels, or with relatives and friends. I'd estimate as many as one hundred and growing. There have been no real hostilities as yet, but I'm keeping a tight rein on our vampires." She glanced down at the paper in her hand, then continued. "None of the tribes are wealthy so I should imagine resources are strained for many."

"Unless we have better contact with the tribes, the hostility part is likely to change."

"I'd bet money on it, Cornelius," Sav said.

Christian sat on the top of the dais and glanced back at his father. "I spoke with his Eminence, Nikolai. He suggested we lay in stores for them. It's one way he develops good will with the tribe on his estate."

"Good idea. See to it, Sav. She should know what will be needed to keep them supplied in food. Offer whatever aid they need. Hopefully it will keep tempers in check until we find out exactly what is going on." A cloud of whitish mist formed in front of the dais, and Mael paused in the middle of his instructions. When Selena appeared in front of him, he smiled wryly. "Good evening, Selena. A pleasure to see you."

"No, it's not, Mael. Since when did you start doing the pretty with me again?" The beautiful, titian-haired, former first formula smiled with her trademark sultriness. In a graceful motion that would put a model to shame, she ascended the steps of the dais to sit on the arm of Mael's throne.

Mael spared a prayer his angel was elsewhere. Selena tended to rub Cian the wrong way with little effort. There was no sign of the wings she'd gained after her failed attempt on Mael's life that ended with her death. Only a few of his closest court members knew she was now the consort of the prince of Heaven.

"I appreciate you helping us out in this situation, Selena, regardless of what you might choose to believe."

She paused to eye him in a questioning manner before a small smile appeared. "You mean that, don't you? It really wasn't a hard decision, dearest. You guys needed me again."

"We're happy to have you here, Selena. Me most of all." Cornelius flashed one of his infamous grins at her.

"I don't doubt it a bit," Selena chuckled. "So fill me in. Michael just said something about a warning from a demon, and Dio said he wanted you there and me here."

"Diocourides has summoned me and Cian to Rome. I'm to be a member of the Inner Circle as an excuse. It's only temporary, and you and Cornelius will be needed to hold down this fort. We also have a potential problem with some were tribes. Sav and Cornelius can fill you in."

"Only back a few seconds and problems already abound." She grimaced, wrapping an arm around Mael's shoulder. "Michael will be keeping an eye on things as well. You don't need to worry. We'll hold your throne in one piece until you get back."

"I'll leave it in everybody's capable hands." Mael stood and headed for the throne room doors. Christian jumped up and joined Mael.

"Do you want me to stay here or join you in Rome, father?"

Mael considered the question as they moved down the hall toward the front stairs. "I want you in Rome with us. We'll be taking Taylor as well. If anything happens, I want you both close."

"We'll have to deal with Nigel." Christian's laugh was light-hearted, but his expression was rueful.

"We can both handle him, child. There will be some things we need to talk about as well. Once we're settled in Rome."

"Look forward to it, pops." Christian winked at Mael before he went his own way in the direction of his room.

* * *

Cian settled in one of the chairs and waited. At least he'd escaped the throne room entirely tonight. Mael, it seemed, had been accosted every five seconds by someone needing something. When the prince finally entered the office, Cian chuckled.

"I'm surprised you managed to get out of there."

"Since I'm leaving for Rome soon, everybody expects me to instantly solve all of their problems before I go." Mael settled on the edge of the desk closest to Cian. "Things went well with Linda, I hope? Please tell me they did. I could use a little good news."

"They did. She was quite happy to know the tribes are welcome here, and the food went a long way in cementing trust, I think. Given her reception, I don't foresee any troubles from them. We just need to keep tabs on the vampires who are likely to protest the weres' presence."

"Sav has my permission to use a harsh hand on any who cause problems, and the rest of my court are aware of it as well. Shouldn't be any trouble there, either." Leaning forward, Mael rested a hand on Cian's shoulder. "I sense something else is bothering you. A subject we should both discuss, and I'll let you go first."

"Am I that transparent?" Cian sighed. "Do you think Cornelius knew about Brandon?"

"I'm sure he knew about Brandon being a first formula. He's fed from Brandon, and it would have been obvious. As to the exact blood line, no, he didn't. He would have come straight to me with information like that."

Cian smiled when Mael began toying with his hair. "I'll admit, that makes me feel a bit better. It's not that I don't trust Cornelius, it's just a bit of a shock to learn something like that." He ran his hand along the outer side of Mael's left thigh. A slight shift of Mael's body gave Cian better access. "Although I have to wonder how they're handling the news."

"He may worry about Triarius' claim on Brandon, but I'm sure the rest won't bother Cornelius. He was never much for politics. I'm more worried about you, my angel. I know how you feel about Aldrich and his ilk."

"Aldrich is dead. Do I like knowing Brandon is of the same bloodline? No. But there's nothing I can do about it. Meeting Triarius was a first. I'd heard rumors, but it's the first time I've ever seen him. I don't know if I trust him or not." More content to focus on his prince than his own issues with rogues, Cian traced his fingers farther along Mael's thigh, moving over the top, to the inside. "And, yes, I know—you're technically a rogue, too. But you're... different."

"The difference has everything to do with the fact you love me." The prince's mouth twitched with a smile. He grabbed Cian's hand and brought it to his lips. "Not exactly an argument that would be accepted in a court of law. As far as Triarius, I trust Dio. He would do nothing to endanger the Romanorum. Neither would Triarius; he hasn't in all the years he's existed."

"I trust Dio, too," Cian said, though a bit distracted. Mael had a knack for doing so, he'd learned.

One finger trailed over Cian's cheek, and the prince's smile became a smirk. "I've been thinking of ditching the London scene and running away to Paris. Care to join me?"

"Mmm..." Cian caught the prince's hand this time and nipped the tip of Mael's index finger. "Sounds good to me. Should I bother packing any clothes?" he teased, rolling his tongue around Mael's fingertip.

"Smart ass. Now what I am sensing? You want something, perhaps? But what could that be?"

"It's been five days," Cian said. "I refuse to wait any longer." He kissed a slow path from Mael's fingertips, over his palm, to the prince's wrist.

A small wound opened across Mael's wrist and pearls of blood welled up. Mael murmured in a soft voice, "Anything you need, my angel."

Eyes drifting shut, Cian began to drink. His head swam with the taste, an addiction only Mael could relieve. The more he had, the stronger the need filled him. He hated going so long without it, but time alone had become a precious commodity for them. The connection between them flared stronger, drawing them into the unique sense of one. Mael's free hand smoothed over Cian's hair and a soft growl filled the scant space between them. Cian licked the wound, then rose. He cupped the back of Mael's head and drew him in for a kiss. With a flick of his tongue, his own blood seeped into Mael's mouth.

Moaning, Cian threaded his fingers through Mael's hair, every nerve in his body firing in response when the prince began to drink. His heart pounded like mad and the sensations rushed through him. One of Mael's hands slipped between them and unfastened Cian's pants. Cian panted into Mael as the prince began stroking him, languid pulls, up and down.

"Mael..."

Mael turned them and pressed Cian back onto the desk. "Don't move."

Cian obeyed. Hell, how could he not? Mael locked the door and returned. He tugged Cian's pants down and off, then knelt on the floor. Propped on his arms, Cian watched as the prince kissed and nipped his way up the inside of his thigh. The closer Mael got, the harder Cian's cock became

The prince's dark blue gaze met Cian's for a brief moment, then Mael sucked him down. Cian fell back onto the desk, hands grasping Mael's head. Mael pulled back up and lifted Cian's legs until they pressed to Cian's chest. A tongue teased him, thrusting in before circling the puckered rim. Cian moaned Mael's name, desperate to feel more.

"Mine," Mael murmured as he worked his way back up Cian's body. At some point, he'd undressed, or at least freed himself. The head of his cock pressed against Cian's ass. "All... mine," he growled, plunging into Cian.

"Mael!" Cian bucked, fingers digging into Mael's biceps. The prince kept the rhythm hard but slow, every stroke ending with a grind of Mael's hips. Cian held on tight, unable to do anything but feel. Mael gripped Cian's cock and pumped it in time to his thrusts. It didn't take long before Cian cried out Mael's name, coming hard enough to take his breath away.

Mael struck Cian's throat without warning. The prince's cock swelled and pulsed, filling Cian with heat. Mael licked the bite wounds closed, then rested his head on Cian's chest.

"Maybe we should have these talks more often," Cian said.

Mael chuckled. "I agree."

Chapter Five

Christian entered the pool area, towel wrapped around his waist. He was due for a bit of relaxation before he had to face his grandfather. His mind still wasn't clear on what to tell Nigel or how much not to say. When he heard splashing, he noticed Taylor for the first time. He hadn't talked to Taylor much since his arrival, but the little he knew about the mortal, he liked.

"Hey, Taylor."

Taylor lifted himself out of the water and smiled. "Hi. I wasn't sure if anyone ever used this thing," he said, gesturing to the pool. "Company would be cool."

"When court is in session, nobody uses it. I came down here to hide out." The towel dropped to Christian's feet and then he dove into the pool.

"Sounds like you're not fond of the court stuff," Taylor said when Christian surfaced.

Christian shook his head and wiped the water from his face. "Oh, I don't mind it most of the time. Mael didn't need me there tonight. So I have some time to kill."

"That's why Cian sent me down here. Actually, he sent me to explore, I think." Taylor leaned back against the edge, arms up on the rim. "I got as far as the mage's workroom."

Christian treaded water near him. "So how have you been doing with all of this? Want to run screaming yet?" A grin softened the words.

"Not until I accidentally stumbled into the workroom. Did you know there's a ghost in there?"

"You'll get used to Aristotle. He's the spirit of Cornelius' crystal ball and he's been around for ages. He loves to steal things. If anything comes up missing, just tell Cornelius." Floating on his back, Christian closed his eyes and waved his arms in a lazy pattern.

"Wait. The crystal ball has a spirit? I thought crystal balls were just... crystal?"

"Not if you want an accurate crystal ball. Or so Cornelius insists."

"I think I'll stick to tarot cards," Taylor laughed.

"So you're a fortune teller? I've some practical magical application I learned from Cornelius. Not as much as he'd liked to teach me, but Nigel doesn't think it has much of a place in my studies."

"Not so much of a fortune teller, but I've been reading the cards since I was ten."

"You should read me. You want to?"

"Sure. It's the one thing I managed to hold onto when my folks kicked me out."

"A few laps first, then the cards." With a laugh, Christian rolled to his stomach and swam away in swift, sure strokes.

Out of the corner of his eye, he saw Taylor catch up and maintain the same momentum. Taylor reached the far edge first, pushed off the wall, and headed back toward the opposite side. In no hurry, Christian followed him and did three laps before he headed to the edge of the pool. He enjoyed the lack of competition between them. He got enough of that from other members of the court. He finally hauled himself up and out, then grabbed his towel to dry off.

"You ready to head upstairs yet?"

Taylor climbed out and his long hair plastered to his chest as he began drying. "Ready when you are," he said, tying the towel around his waist.

"Wow, no wonder Cian picked you." Christian led the way out of the pool room. "You're in luck, too. I guess you'll be changed while we're in Rome. No question of your position with Diocourides' backing."

"So why is it no wonder that he picked me?" Taylor asked as they headed toward his room.

"He must be attracted to you, right?" Nobody blinked an eye when the two of them strode through the halls clad only in suits and towels.

"Nope. From what I've seen, it would take an act of God to pull him away from the prince. Besides, I'm just another guy. Especially around here."

After he opened the door, Christian blocked the entrance. He turned and stared at Taylor. "That's complete and utter bullshit. Just another guy isn't why Cian picked you. If that were true, this place would be littered with them. My father hasn't created any others since he created me. Not since Amael."

Taylor blinked at him in surprise. "Christian, before Cian found me, I was a homeless gay guy surviving by whoring himself out. I'm glad Cian brought me here, but I'm still not sure why he did it."

"Well, maybe you need to ask him. I don't know a lot about the guy, but he strikes me as the hard to get close to type. There must be something about you for him to trust you like this." He entered the room and closed the door after Taylor followed him in. "As for my father, I'd be willing to bet he already knows you inside and out. He's found you worthy of his blood. You might want to talk to him, too."

"Trust me, I intend to." Taylor opened the top middle drawer of his dresser and pulled out a small rectangle of black velvet tied with a gold braided cord. "Have a seat," he said, gesturing to the bed.

"Since my father has accepted you, and I trust his instinct, you're good with me." Christian flashed him another friendly grin as he sat at the edge of the bed. He liked the guy, no doubt about it. He felt at ease around Taylor and trusted him.

Taylor sat near the headboard. "Thanks. It's nice to be able to relax without worrying about... well... other things." He set the rectangle on the bed and untied the cord. Then he spread out the cloth, velvet side up, and shuffled the dragon-decorated cards. "Have you ever had a reading?"

"No." As he watched Taylor work with the cards, Christian stretched out on his side to get more comfortable.

Taylor set the deck down. "Cut it three ways, any way you want."

Christian picked up several cards, set them into a pile, then picked a few more and did the same.

Taylor gathered them once more. "I'm doing a general reading of your near future. We can do more detailed readings later, if you want. The first card is your distant past." He flipped over the top card, The Tower. "You've had many trials and disruptions throughout your life."

"That would be a mild way to put it." Good humored, he eyed the cards then Taylor.

"Believe me, I know the feeling." Taylor turned over the next card, The Devil. "Your recent past has elements of a domineering presence, someone or something who forces changes that may or may not be good."

"I'd say that would be Nigel since Mael's dominating was in the not so recent past."

"The next one is the present." Taylor placed the card down and smiled. "Ten of Cups. The beginning of friendship, happiness."

Christian reached over and flicked the end of Taylor's hair. "I won't argue with that one."

Color crept into Taylor's cheeks and he gave Christian a smile. "Next one, near future." He flipped it over, the smile fading almost immediately. "Nine of Swords," he muttered. "Loss, desolation..."

"That doesn't sound good." Christian looked down at the cards, wishing he could read them himself.

"I'll say. Just be careful." Taylor pulled out the last card. Just before he flipped it over, another card landed on his lap. He glanced down, one eyebrow lifting. "Knight of Wands. A friend." He grinned and then finished turning over the last card for Christian. He nearly dropped the deck. "The Lovers... beginning of a new relationship, possibly a romance."

"Think I prefer the friend. They're harder to come by." Christian grimaced. "You have to be careful who you pick around here. Way too many want the perks of our positions. So watch yourself."

"I've noticed," Taylor said as he gathered the cards. "Well, there's your reading. Not exactly the most... positive one I've done, but hey, anything can change."

"Most of it sounded good to me. Thanks for the reading. Now back to you. What do you think of everything so far?"

Christian rolled onto his back and stretched out on the bed, the towel still draped around him.

Taylor remained silent for a few seconds. "I think I'm enjoying it quite a bit, actually."

"I was hoping you would. It's nice having you around. Somebody I can talk to who I don't have to worry about the position thing. Yours will be the same as mine. Just as prestigious." Growing serious for a moment, Christian added, "You know I'm not jealous of you or anything like that, don't you? I'm not like Amael. Not one bit."

"Same here. I haven't had anyone I could call a real friend in... well, a long time." Taylor put his cards on the velvet and folded it, tying it closed again. "Who is Amael?"

"He was Mael's oldest when I was created. It's a long story. The short version is he didn't like me much and wanted me out of the way."

Taylor winced. "Something tells me that didn't turn out well for Amael..."

"No, it didn't. Mael might be worried about the jealousy thing, but I'm not really the type. He is, but I'm not." Christian shrugged. "I won't try to hurt you or anything like that. I like you."

This time, Taylor definitely blushed. "Thanks. The feeling is quite mutual."

"Didn't want you running around thinking I had it in for you." If anything, Christian found he liked Taylor a bit too much. Overall, though, he was grateful to have a friend he knew he could trust.

"Nah. There's just something about you." Taylor tipped his head a little, his hair a bit less damp and looser as it brushed over his chest. "I trust you. That might sound odd, considering we just met, but..."

"I know what you mean." When he rolled to his side, Christian offered Taylor his hand. "I have the feeling we'll be good friends."

* * *

Taylor couldn't get his reading for Christian out of his mind. He'd thought the guy was gorgeous the moment they'd first met, but a romance? Somehow, Taylor just couldn't wrap his brain around that one. A rumbling stomach turned his thoughts to less perplexing matters, namely food. He managed to find the kitchen, surprised to see Cian sitting at the bar on one of the two large islands.

"I wondered where you ran off to. Hungry?" Cian asked before taking a bite from the steak in front of him.

"Angels eat?"

Cian laughed and nodded. "We don't really have to, but the first time I tasted human food, I was hooked. I eat for pleasure, not hunger."

Taylor smiled and pulled up a stool on the other side of the island. "Food sounds good. Especially after a swim."

"Ah, so you found the pool." Cian got up and fixed Taylor a plate full of steak and roasted potatoes. He set it down and took his seat once more. "I haven't been down there yet, believe it or not."

The first bite of steak nearly had Taylor moaning. "Wow," he mumbled.

Cian grinned. "Mael spares no expense."

"I noticed."

"Have you been able to catch him yet?"

"Not yet. How do you two ever get a moment's peace together? It seems like everybody wants his attention."

"We have to steal the time every once in a while," Cian said. "But, he's a prince and has a city to look over. It's his duty and that's something I know quite a bit about."

"Are you something like a prince?"

Cian nearly choked on a sip of water. "Hardly. I was a general. Well, technically, I still am, I suppose."

"So you've been in battles?"

"Many, the last being one of... legendary proportions," Cian said. One eyebrow lifting, Taylor took a bite of potato. Cian chuckled softly. "I led an army in the war against Samael."

"Who?"

"You know him by the name of Lucifer."

Taylor's jaw nearly hit the floor. "How old are you?"

Cian seemed to think for a moment before answering. "A little over three thousand, I think. I sort of lost track."

"You..." Taylor swallowed. "Holy shit. I mean..." Cian laughed. "Wow. Just... The things you've seen have got to be off the charts."

"I've been on Earth for the past several hundred years," Cian said. "I've seen every facet of humanity, most of which I would care not to see again."

"Were you around for the Crusades, stuff like that?"

"Oh, yes. My first human lover was a Crusader. His name was Richard, though not the king, before you ask."

"What happened to him?"

"I found him mortally wounded at his final battle. Unable to save him, I had no choice but to watch him die in my arms. I refused to love another mortal after that."

"I'm sorry..."

"It's okay. That was a long time ago, and while I still think of him, my heart and soul belong to Mael now."

"How does an angel come to terms with being gay?"

Cian pushed his empty plate to the side and sipped his water. "We don't share the same views and hangups as humans. Love, and even sex, are acts of the soul for us. It's why, when an angel gives his or her love, it is for eternity." He tilted his head a little and studied Taylor. "How did your parents find out about you?"

Taylor toyed with a piece of steak and sighed. "One of my teachers at school found a poem I'd written about a guy I liked. She took it to the principal, who called my folks. It wasn't pretty. I lived in an uptight community, and being gay was highly discouraged, to say the least."

"Did you leave?"

"Not willingly. My mother didn't want me to go, but the alternative was therapy to 'cure' me. Given a choice between repressing who I was, or leaving and being able to at least live as a gay man, I walked out."

Cian's hand covered his and squeezed gently. "You know that is something you will never have to worry about again."

"I know." Taylor met Cian's blue gaze and smiled. "Thank you. Can I ask another question?"

"Of course."

"Why did you pick me?"

Cian studied him in silence for a few seconds before speaking. "There is a light in you, a brightness in your soul. I couldn't let that die out. I knew the moment I first saw you, before I ever approached you about coming with me."

"What do you mean, a light?"

"Innocence." At Taylor's raised eyebrow, Cian chuckled softly. "It has nothing do with anything torrid. There isn't an evil, or even unpleasant, thing about you. Your soul is pure, whether your mind and body are not. In essence, it was your soul—the very depths of who you really are—that made me realize you were the one."

"Wow..." Taylor didn't know what to say. No one had ever uttered such things about him. "I don't know how to thank you beyond... thank you."

Cian smiled. "You're very welcome."

Chapter Six

"Hey, Daddy-o, got some words of advice for you."

A brow went up at Christian's choice of greeting, but Mael only smiled. "And that would be?"

Christian sat down and propped his feet on Mael's legs. "You guys need to talk to Taylor. The poor kid doesn't even know why you two picked him." Blunt and to the point, that was Christian in a nutshell.

"I thought Cian had spoken to him about our choice. I'll have to remind him and talk to Taylor myself."

Mael fell silent, studying his only child. He saw beneath the oh-so-casual surface to the depths beneath. Most of what he sensed in Christian was uncertainty toward himself. There wasn't an ounce of resentment or ill will toward Taylor. In fact, the opposite seemed to be true, which relieved Mael.

While Christian might not be too sure of his own place, he didn't begrudge one for Taylor.

Darkness festered in Christian, however, and Mael knew it'd been fostered by his father, Nigel. He felt the anger and bitterness buried deep. It was long past time for Christian to return to his proper home. Mael had his fair share of guilt over the decades for letting his father train Christian.

"Have you thought of remaining here with me, Christian?"

Shocked would have been a good word for Christian's expression. "Why would you want that?"

"You're my son, and you belong with me, not my father. I should have brought you back long ago." Mael offered no excuse since there were none. Time had gotten away from both of them, and he could see the damage it'd done to Christian.

All of his sudden, Christian became uncomfortable and dropped his legs to the floor. "I-I-I don't know. I just wanted to talk to you about Taylor. He's awfully clueless about all of this, and that doesn't seem fair."

Mael allowed the subject change, willing to give Christian time to consider what he said. "I'll speak with both of them." A knock at the door drew Mael attention. "Come in."

"Your Excellency, Sav has news for you about the weres."

"Don't let it become too late because everything else interfered, Mael." Christian stood and bowed.

Sav entered as Christian left. "Your Excellency." She stopped in front of Mael and bowed. "I've received reports from Cudham and Hadley Wood about several were deaths."

Mael felt the sting of the Christian's words, but Sav's statement distracted him. "What's going on, Sav?"

"So far we've discovered five deaths and twenty-three weres hospitalized in both areas. The death reports list traces of Silver Asperia in all the victims."

"Silver Asperia?"

"Cornelius would know about it, your Excellency."

"Cornelius attend me in my study." Mael nodded to Sav to continue.

"Several vets in the area have found large amounts in the wildlife weres hunt for food as well as in many of the farm animals. It doesn't harm the animals, but it does affect the weres."

A dark hole appeared on the wall nearest Mael, and Cornelius walked into the room. "You rang?"

"Silver Asperia. What do you know of it?"

"It's a very rare magical flower. Why?" The magician sat in the chair beside Mael and helped himself to a glass of blood wine from the nearby decanter.

"Used to kill weres?"

"Oh, is that what's been doing it?" He paused, one finger nudging his spectacles higher on his nose. "Not very cost effective, Mael. The time and money that goes into growing Silver Asperia is beyond most sorcerers. It would certainly thin the were population, though."

"Somebody is using it to poison the animal populace in Cudham and Hadley Wood," Sav explained. "It's why the weres have fled into the city. They are looking for a safer food supply. The cause isn't general knowledge right now because the tribes are scrambling to keep it all contained."

"Sav, set up a meeting with Linda Ellsworth for me. At her convenience."

"Yes, your Excellency." She bowed to Mael, then left to make the appointment.

"So tell me about Silver Asperia."

"I've never heard of anyone using it to poison weres. Not a bright choice if you ask me. It costs more than fifty thousand pounds just to maintain a few of the flowers. They are temperamental to the extreme and require several magical compounds to facilitate growth. But once fully grown, I suppose the crushed petals could be added to the food ingested by other animals. Any were eating a tainted animal would get an unhealthy dose of something similar to silver in their system. It would be an expensive, but effective way to eliminate weres without harming humans."

"Who in your circle could grow it?"

"I have a couple of plants myself, and I know of only two others who have the time and money for Silver Asperia. I'll check around for you, Mael." A portal formed on the nearest wall, and Cornelius stood to take his leave.

"Thank you. Any information you can get as soon as possible will be appreciated."

After the mage left, Mael set aside the book in his lap. His attention was taken by too many other thoughts to be able to enjoy reading. He stood, tightened the tie of his black dressing gown, and decided to try for a few peaceful moments in his garden. The shadows he called up swarmed around him and before he stepped out of them, he sensed someone else in his private garden.

No one else entered his sanctuary except for his gardener Samson, Cian, and Christian. The moment Mael realized it was Taylor; he relaxed and watched the young man in silence. Most likely, the boy had wandered into the garden by accident. There were no obvious signs to keep others out, though all knew not to set foot in the walled enclosure.

A luminous glow from the night-blooming Blue Venus lit Taylor's face as he crouched to get a better look at it. Powerful magic kept the outer cold at bay and maintained the immediate area in a warm climate for the animals and vegetation.

He wasn't aware of Mael, and for the moment, Mael kept it that way. The surface was easy enough for Mael to read. The mortal had had a hard life. Some of the choices he'd made were questionable. None of it interested Mael in the least. Of course, there were emotional scars, but time and care would ease those.

It required a bit more effort to search beneath the outer debris clouding the boy's essence.

The moment he sensed it and realized what it was, he smiled to himself. It was no wonder what had gotten his angel's attention so completely. As he searched within Taylor, it fair shone to Mael's mind. It was as the heart of a child, so blindingly brilliant. Undiminished loyalty, love, and belief were as much a part of the mortal as breathing.

He had already made up his mind to accept the child for Cian's sake, but he should have known better. Only his angel would find such a rare jewel as this one. When he stepped from the darkness to alert Taylor to his presence, he coughed softly to gain Taylor's attention.

"Hello?" Taylor turned, only briefly nervous before he seemed to realize it was only Mael. He smiled. "I'm not sure how I ended up here, probably a wrong turn. It's... amazing, though. It's nice to be able to enjoy nature without knowing I have to sleep in it."

"It's my private garden, Taylor, but you, Cian, and Christian are welcome here as well. Sleeping outside is something you'll only have to do if you want to now. How have you been settling in?"

"Thanks." Taylor sat down on one of the stone benches that stood near the fountain. "Pretty good, actually. I've never seen a place this big—or this nice, much less been in one. I found the pool, too. Christian and I had fun doing some laps, and I did a reading for him." He blushed a little, then laughed softly. "I'm not used to having someone I can call a true friend. He's... well, he's really cool."

"He is most definitely an original." Mael chuckled. "He seems to consider you a friend as well, and he took me to task earlier for not talking to you about the reason you're here."

"I talked to Cian," Taylor said. "He told me he wanted a son, and that he'd been watching me for a while. He said it's my soul. I'll take his word for it. I still don't see what he saw, but I'm glad he did."

A friendly warmth surrounded Mael as he settled beside Taylor. More than a little aware of how intimidating he could be, he toned down that aspect of himself for Taylor's sake. "You can take my word for it, too. I was prepared to accept whatever choice Cian made, but I find you have an exceptional quality that isn't easily defined. It is unmistakable, and I'm sure you'll do me proud as my son."

Taylor definitely blushed, no doubt about it. "Thank you. I..." He swallowed and stared off into space for a few seconds. "I don't know how much Cian told you, but it's not pretty. For a long time, I missed having a place to live. After a while, I think I just grew numb. Being here, though... it's proof that there's a difference between a place to live, and a real home."

"None here will judge you for your past. Few of us had stellar ones. This is your home for as long as you need it." Mael patted Taylor's hand with a laugh. "I should imagine even if London were to tumble down around our ears, Cian would spirit us safely to his tower. Cian, Christian, and I are now your family. Or as Christian would probably say, you are stuck with us now."

Taylor laughed. "Oh! Speaking of Cian, did you know he's over three thousand years old? And that he commanded an army?"

It relieved him to see Taylor had no problem relaxing around him. He commented with a sly grin, "Considering I'm only a third of that, it makes him a cradle robber."

Taylor looked him up and down, then grinned. "You know, he does look older than you."

Mael did his best not to snicker but couldn't help it. "You should mention that to him."

"I'll pass," Taylor laughed. "He's a general. He has a sword... and armor. Have you ever seen it? What does it look like?"

"It's magnificent and gold, but I really didn't pay much attention to it." He knew something in his expression would give him away, but he couldn't help that either. He did remember the interlude with a fond smile.

One eyebrow lifting, Taylor said, "I really don't want to know, do I?"

Mael had to laugh again. "No, I wouldn't think so. But I can change the subject by telling you if you ever mention my age for any reason, it's officially only five hundred."

"Something tells me that's just the 'public' answer." Tilting his head a little, Taylor studied him for a moment. "How old are you, really? I promise I won't say a word."

"Well over a thousand, but a lie keeps my enemies on their toes. It's easier to underestimate me, which I've always encouraged. For the first five centuries, most believed I was my father's ghoul. A ghoul wasn't considered as much of a threat. Vampires weren't as civilized in certain matters as they are now."

"Can I ask you a question?"

"You may ask whatever you want, Taylor."

"Christian told me about ghouls. Cian isn't a vampire, so is he your ghoul?"

There was no reason for Taylor not to know the truth. "Yes, he drinks my blood. As I do his. Technically, he is a ghoul, but it doesn't extend his life span as it would for a mortal."

"Does an angel's blood taste different?"

"It is far more powerful than human or even vampire blood. It has a flavor all its own I would be hard pressed to describe."

Taylor seemed to think on it. "I haven't seen his wings yet. I wonder if I'll have any, since I'll have vampire and angel blood. What do his wings look like?"

"You should ask him to show them to you. I doubt he'd mind. It's very possible you will since you'll have traits from both of us. His wings are sapphire blue."

"I thought all angel wings were white. Now I'm really curious," Taylor said. "By the way, completely off-topic, but where in the world did you find such an awesome household cook? You can't eat... or can you? Cian said he doesn't have to, but he enjoys it."

Somewhat bemused by all the questions, Mael did his best to answer. "Edward is the highest paid chef in this country, he had better be awesome and then some. I can eat when I wish to appear more human, but it takes magical ability."

"The man should be sainted," Taylor laughed. "His steaks are... wow."

"Feel free to bother the man any time you wish. He has a standing order to take care of you. You're one of the few who are allowed to make demands of him."

"I'll remember that. Maybe I can take full advantage of his cooking skills before I get turned. Speaking of... how is it done?"

Mael paused for a moment to find the words to explain the process in a way Taylor would understand. "Cornelius, my mage, and the father of all vampires, Diocourides, are working on combining Cian's blood with my own and the formula for creation. It's a delicate process or so I'm given to understand, but the two have been gleefully at it for some time." He gave Taylor a serious look. "There is some risk to this. I wouldn't let them proceed if you didn't understand that part. They believe with the addition of Cian's blood, it may negate some small part of the risk. When it comes time, I will drain you near death, then you will be given the formula. None of it will hurt; I'll make sure it won't."

"Has anyone ever done it? Combine two different types of blood, I mean."

"To my knowledge, it has never been done. Vampires consider themselves to be superior creatures and none I know of would infuse their blood with another like this. Nor do any have access to angel blood."

"So... I'm a guinea pig," Taylor laughed. "This should be interesting. Oh, just to give you a heads-up, because I'm sure you've noticed by now, I have ADHD—you know, attention deficit hyperactivity disorder. Ninety percent of the time, my brain won't shut up and my mouth has a bad habit of running away. And I'm babbling..."

"Indeed you are a guinea pig. You can speak to Cornelius about the particulars if you need. He'd be delighted to fill you in." He reached over to pat Taylor's cheek in an affectionate touch. "I'm not having any trouble keeping up with you. You may babble all you wish."

"Lord, don't tell me that. There's no knowing what will come out of my mouth sometimes."

"I don't mind at all. Feel free to be yourself." He stood then waited for Taylor. "We should go inside since it's near time for my court session."

Taylor got up and joined him. "Yeah. Maybe I can hunt down Christian again."

* * *

Sav had arranged for Mael to meet with Linda Ellsworth in a neutral place. He'd had to cut short the court meeting to arrive on time. As he entered the church, he greeted Father Shepard with a polite bow.

"Good evening, Father Shepard. Cian said to tell you hello, as well."

"Welcome, Prince Black. Tell him hello for me. I'm pleased you're as interested in taking care of this problem as the church is."

"I would prefer good ties with the were community. It would make life easier for all us."

Linda entered the church from vestibule. Father Shepard watched them both in silence. He was only there as a witness and mediator, if necessary. "I was told you'd put the word out to protect my brethren from your kind," Linda said. "Much appreciated, Prince Black."

"As is your help in keeping were tempers in check." He smiled at her and offered his hand.

She took his hand with a smile of her own. To his surprise, he detected no signs of wariness. "I was also told the first of the food supplies would be arriving later today. Your generosity is beyond appreciated since we have more people arriving everyday. Very few can afford any of this."

"Just let Sav know whatever you need, and, please, call me Mael." It was a gesture of personal good will on his part to offer the informality of first names.

"I'd be delighted. You can call me Linda."

He inclined his head in gracious acknowledgment. "I have been called to Rome, Linda. While I'm gone, Sav and Cornelius will handle everything you need. I've also given Sav a free hand to punish any vampires who cause problems for your tribes."

"I've met her. She looks like she could kick some vamp ass and not break a sweat."

"She does excel in her chosen position." Since Sav was his assassin, it was best not to mention the woman's full capabilities. "And please don't hesitate to let one of them know if you need help. The sooner we can solve your dilemma, the sooner safety and peace will return to your brethren."

"Many of them are scared. Some of our food supplies have been poisoned, and nobody knows who or why. You know it's pretty bad when we're willing to accept food from vampires." The smile on her lips lessened the harshness of the words. "No offense intended, but we've never been the best of friends."

"I know our first formula of the United States, Nikolai, has close ties with a were tribe who live on his estate. I've learned a few things from him and would like to see a change in the relationship between our kinds, Linda. I have no problem with a larger were population in London, though I know many prefer hunting space in more rural areas."

"That is generous of you. I know a few who would prefer city life, but they have hesitated due to the heavy number of vamps here. I'll take it under consideration."

"You may trust my people to help you as much as you need." He offered his hand to her again in farewell. She shook it.

"Once we're settled in the warehouse you provided, I'll be in closer contact with them. Thank you again, Mael."

Chapter Seven

Rome, Home of Prince Nigel

The rumors and innuendo coming from London were enough to disturb Nigel more than he had ever been. He took a great deal of pride in his son, Mael, and the position Mael had gained for himself. However, to have taken up with a vampire-hunting sorcerer? Nigel was appalled at Mael's lack of consideration for his family and their prestigious line. None of his children had given him such cause for concern until now. Neither Carolina nor Justin had ever indulged in this kind of outrageous behavior.

He had to wonder if sorcery had been used to enthrall Mael. As his eldest, Mael should know better, and it would sadden him beyond words if it were true that his child had so far forgotten himself. The aroma of his cigar soothed his mood somewhat as he took deliberate breaths to smoke it.

When the door opened and Christian entered, Nigel felt an inward contentment. The boy had turned out far better than Nigel had thought he would. One day he would be as proud of Christian as he was most times with Mael.

"Good evening, grandfather." Christian performed a respectful bow, then sat in the chair beside Nigel.

Nigel let a moment slip by as he studied his grandson. "I've heard some disturbing things regarding London and your father. I assume Mael and his..." He couldn't bring himself say 'companion.' "... sorcerer have arrived in Rome."

"They are settling in the Romanorum right now. Diocourides has placed Mael in his wing." Christian shifted in his seat, which wasn't at all like him.

Though the news of his son landing such a prestigious position in Diocourides' own quarters touched him with pride, Nigel narrowed his gaze on Christian. "There is more," he said, fastening a shrewd gaze on his grandson as he took another puff from the cigar.

"I don't believe it's as bad as you think, grandfather. I think Cian is a good man, and my father loves him a great deal." As he spoke, Christian held Nigel's gaze with a steady one of his own. "And I don't believe Cian used any kind of magic on Mael."

"It is unbecoming of someone of my blood to stoop to such a thing. Cavorting with a known hunter and sorcerer..." Nigel stubbed out the cigar, the conversation topic quelling any comfort it gave. "Mael has clearly forgotten the importance of his lineage."

Christian still looked unconvinced before his expression smoothed to one of neutrality. "As you say, grandfather. They are very close, and I doubt they will tire of each other any time soon. Mael refuses to allow any kind of physical relationship with me again."

Nigel pondered the tidbit of information. He could work it to his advantage—anything to get rid of his son's dalliance with such an unworthy recipient. "What can you tell me about your father's... favored past-time? I want details on this man."

"His favorite pastime involves his hands on Cian." There might have been a bit of a spark of jealousy in Christian's eyes. "Cian's favorite pastime is the same. Make of that what you will."

Nigel suppressed the urge to smile. "And what of Cian? What is he like, where is he from?"

"He's from Wales, and a decent guy from what I've seen. So is Taylor, the one Mael and Cian have chosen for their son." For the first time, a genuine smile appeared.

Nigel nodded. "I've heard Taylor's name, but know nothing more. What have you learned about him?"

"As a mortal, he has no social standing. But from what I know of him, I'd bet serious money he'll make you proud, grandfather. There is something special about him." Clearly, Christian believed what he said.

Nigel did smile this time. "You seem fond of him."

Christian fastened his gaze on the floor near Nigel's feet. "He's becoming a good friend, grandfather. It's nice to have someone who isn't influenced by who I am."

The admission surprised Nigel. He found himself quite interested in hearing more about this new potential progeny. "You hold a high standing, but I'm glad you've found a friend."

"Diocourides approves of him as well, which, you know, will carry great weight with everyone. I believe father choose very wisely this time. There is no jealousy between me and Taylor. That will avoid the problem Amael gave us."

"Jealousy can have devastating effects," Nigel said. He remembered well enough the end result of Amael's jealousy over Christian. "I am assuming then that your father has petitioned formally?"

"Yes, and nobody expects any refuting of the petition. I don't believe Diocourides would consider it much if there were."

"And what do you think of this? It is obvious you enjoy Taylor's friendship, but he is set to become Mael's son as well."

"He adores Mael, grandfather." Christian chuckled. "And father is already bonding with him. There's no mistaking it. I don't even think Taylor is much concerned about turning."

"Yes..." Nigel leaned forward slightly, catching Christian's gaze. "But how do *you* feel about it?"

Christian blinked. "I'm glad to have a friend and a new brother, grandfather. We get along very well, and I'm really happy when we do things together."

Nigel relaxed back in his chair once more. "As I said, I am glad you've found a friend. Perhaps Mael chose better than he did with Amael."

As Mael walked down the hall, he noticed there were far more ancient antiques than he remembered from his more youthful nights. And those were just the vampires, not the antiquities. He spotted more than a few he knew had been created close to the same time he had been. Were more of the old ones haunting the halls of the Romanorum for their own reasons, or was his memory faulty? The older ones were set in their ways, and many paid no more than lip service to the current laws of the Romanorum. However, even they realized toying with humans wasn't worth a death penalty.

The office Dio had set him up in was even more luxurious then his own back in London. If anything, older vampires loved to display their wealth. Even though it really wasn't Diocourides' style, the father of all vampires allowed it. Settled behind his desk, Mael read over the reports Sav had compiled for him.

"I admit," Cian said as he entered from the room connected to the office, "I never pegged Dio as the type to go for opulence."

"It keeps a lot of the others happy if they can display prestige." Since Mael was guilty of the same sin at times, he couldn't say much about it.

Cian chuckled and sat in the chair opposite Mael. "What did Dio have to say?"

"There is some indication the Holy Sons might be operating once again. You probably had some experiences with them before they were outlawed. There have been a few reports of staked vampires left out in the open and threatening notices sent to others."

Brow wrinkling, Cian shook his head. "Who would be stupid enough to start them back up again?"

"The church is claiming none of their own are involved, and there's no proof they have anything to do with it. It seems they want as little to do with that part of their past as we do."

"Makes me wonder if it's tied somehow to whatever is stirring up the weres in London," Cian mused. "Does Dio have any ideas?"

"He's having the stakings investigated, and Sav tells me things are calm in London. There have been no more deaths or anybody hospitalized, and most of the tainted meat has been destroyed." Mael propped his feet on the desk and leaned back in the chair.

"Lee's right there with her, then. He won't let her out of his sight for long these days." Cian tipped his head slightly. "Something else is on your mind. What is it, *cariad*?"

"Nigel has been making several demands of me. I expected it when Diocourides asked us to come here." Closing his eyes, Mael sighed, fingers rubbing his temples. "The man knows every damn button to push when it comes to me."

Cian got up and stood behind Mael. He began massaging Mael's shoulders, working out the stiffness. "Dare I ask what he wants?"

Mael tipped his head back and eyed Cian with a smile. "He wants me to get rid of you. A vampire-hunting sorcerer is not a fit companion for his blood line. I expected his tirade and never thought I would get the man to see sense, but I'd forgotten how didactic he could be."

One eyebrow lifting, Cian let out a short laugh. "When Hell freezes over."

"Likewise, my angel. Nigel has always ruled his family with the proverbial iron fist, and he doesn't like to let go as he should. Until now, it wasn't much of a problem, but being here is aggravating it."

Cian rounded Mael and straddled his lap. "Anything I can do? Send a legion after him? Call up a favor or two from grateful demons? Borrow Michael's sword again?"

Mael couldn't help but grin. "I wish I could say yes to all of the above, but Diocourides would have my head if the seat of Rome went up for grabs."

"Oh, well... I tried. Besides, your head is mine. Both of them."

"Don't you two ever take a break?"

"You'd think in the hallowed halls of the Romanorum we'd be safe," Christian quipped as he and Taylor walked into the office.

"Have either of you ever heard of knocking?" Cian grumbled.

Taylor laughed. "Have you ever heard of a lock?"

"Good one." Christian gave Taylor a high-five as they stopped in front of the desk.

Mael laughed and pinched Cian's ass. "I promise I'll ravage you later."

Cian squirmed, then gave Mael an unapologetic grin. "I'm holding you to that."

"I introduced Taylor around to a few he should know. Got anything else for me, pops?"

"I would suggest you stay close to me for the time being, Christian," Mael said. "Use me for an excuse as to why you're so busy." For the briefest moment, Mael felt a touch of unease when Christian glanced at him.

Christian broke out in a grin. "Oh, come on. I can handle the old man. You worry too much. Besides, I promised to take Taylor out and do some sightseeing."

It didn't exactly ease Mael's worry, but he hid it for the time being. "Just be careful."

Taylor glanced between Mael and Christian. "You two are doing that mind-talking thing, aren't you?"

"Nah, I know he's seen Grandfather, and Mael worries too much all the time."

"I expect you to tell me if there is ever a problem, Christian. Nigel isn't the easiest creature to bear," Mael gently reminded him.

"Neither are you, dear old dad, but I love you anyway." Christian appeared determined to make light of the whole thing.

"Come on." Taylor tugged on Christian's coat sleeve. "You promised me hours of amusement."

"And we're off. Let me know if you need me for anything official." The words were barely out before Taylor dragged him away.

When the door closed, Cian turned back to Mael. "Christian doesn't take Nigel too seriously, I see."

"Oh, he does. He just doesn't want me to worry, but I know more than the boy gives me credit for."

Arms draping over Mael's shoulders, Cian toyed with the prince's hair, his fingers skimming along the back of Mael's neck. "Do you think Nigel would risk doing anything openly?"

"He would find others and risk nothing, Cian, and it troubles me deeply." There was no way to hide everything from his lover, but some of the details Mael preferred to leave unsaid. "I should have made arrangements for Christian to come back with me."

"What aren't you telling me?"

"I am worried about whatever it is the old man is plotting. He could have given Machiavelli lessons in the art. Nigel is too powerful to simply dismiss. Diocourides can control the worst of the man's excesses, but Nigel can still cause significant trouble. Best to watch your back at all times, love."

"Great," Cian sighed. "Is there any good news since we got here?"

"We're still together and always will be. No matter what is thrown at us." Mael leaned forward enough to press a light kiss to his angel's lips. "That's about as good as it's going to get for the time being."

Cian didn't let Mael go, but instead deepened the kiss. "I'm locking the door," he murmured when he drew back. He got up and made sure the door was locked, then pulled Mael toward the bedroom. "No arguing. Just let me love you while we have the chance."

Given that they'd had little time to themselves lately, Mael wasn't about to protest. He let Cian lead him into the bedroom, his gaze fixated on the leather pants in front of him. Cian rarely—if ever—wore anything but his favorite leather, and Mael had absolutely no intentions of changing the man. Not when he had such sights to look forward to every day.

Cian stopped at the bed and began undressing Mael, the look in the angel's eyes hungry. Mael's shirt barely had time to drop to the floor before Cian knelt and worked his dress pants open. Mael remained silent, one hand on his lover's golden hair, as Cian's tongue drew a sensuous path up the length of his cock. When Cian reached the tip, he sucked it into his mouth.

Mael shuddered and gripped the bedpost with his free hand. His other tightened in Cian's hair. "Yes..."

Cian held onto Mael's hips, encouraging him to move. He thrust in and out slowly, utterly entranced by the image of his length sliding between an angel's lips. His movements sped up as need strengthened. Mael didn't know how long he could last, not like this. Then Cian released him.

Mael opened his mouth to protest, but Cian simply grinned and turned him around. With one hand on the small of Mael's back, Cian bent him forward over the bed. Mael didn't bottom often, but when he did, Cian always made damn sure he would never forget it.

"Cian..."

His cheeks spread apart and a wickedly sensual tongue teased him. Mael groaned. He gave up standing and knelt on the bed, his head pillowed on his arms. Cian chuckled softly and went back to his favorite form of torment. The angel's tongue pushed into Mael's body, then withdrew. Over and over, with little flicks in between, it drove Mael insane. It didn't take long before he broke his own silence. One hand beneath him, he stroked his cock and moaned as Cian worked two long fingers inside him.

"Please..."

"Are you ready for me, my prince?" Cian teased, nipping Mael's right cheek while twisting and spreading his fingers.

"Yes," Mael growled. "Now."

Cian pulled out his fingers. "As you wish." A few seconds later, the slick head of his cock pressed against Mael's entrance, but he didn't push any farther. "How do you want it?"

"Just fuck me," Mael ground out through gritted teeth.

Without another word, Cian's fingers dug into Mael's hips and the hard length filled Mael in one swift thrust. Mael barely bit back a shout and had little time to catch his breath before Cian started fucking him hard and fast. He jerked Mael backward with every stroke; Mael knew he wouldn't last.

"Cian." He fisted his own cock once more and pumped it in time to Cian's movements. "Fuck... !" Head thrown back, Mael's entire body seized when he came.

Cian moved faster, then froze, gasping and grinding his cock into Mael. Mael rode the pulsing heat until it stopped, then he dropped onto the bed, Cian on top of him.

"Remind me why I don't bottom more often?" he panted.

Cian laughed, puffs of warm breath tickling Mael's neck. "Because I adore feeling you inside me."

Mael smiled and rested his head sideways, enough to see his angel's face. "You certainly won't hear me complaining either way."

Chapter Eight

"Wow." Taylor stopped in the hallway and stared at the reliefs on the walls. He'd never seen anything like them in his life. Each one depicted a different scene, ranging from everyday life to war to sex. He shook his head. "Maybe I should've paid more attention in art class," he muttered, studying one particular relief of a group of naked people—men and women—loving each other in various combinations.

"Ancient history class, actually," Christian said, appearing almost out of nowhere beside him. "You should get Mael to tell you some tales of the old days. I love to tease the old man about his age."

Taylor grinned over at him. "Believe me, if they had stuff like this..." He pointed to the love scene. "... every guy in art class would've passed with flying colors."

"This is classic art, Taylor. Most definitely too high-brow for drooling youth." Christian smirked at Taylor, then grabbed his arm to pull him down the hall.

"You certainly nailed the guys in art class," Taylor laughed. "Taking me on a tour?"

"After our thoroughly modern night last night, it's time for the past. You have your choice of: The antiques of Dio's youth—dawn of time stuff, Mael's youth—not quite as old as dirt but close, my youth—war at its worst, or just the antiques who live here."

Taylor chuckled. "Surprise me. I'm all yours."

"Mammoths were roaming in Dio's time, but he disputes that with me. There's a lot of gold and precious junk, though.

Come on, I'll show you the temple first." With a grand gesture, Christian led the way.

"Sounds good to me."

The halls weren't empty, and many others scurried to and fro on their duties. Several vampires, quite obvious in importance from the way they carried themselves, were standing around one gentleman, listening in silence. Christian pinched Taylor to get his attention.

"Grandfather," Christian said. "Nigel, prince of Rome."

As they passed, Nigel bowed his head. Cold, pale blue eyes gazed for a moment at both of them. For the briefest moment, Taylor met Nigel's gaze. He shivered as chill ran through him.

"I don't think he likes me much," Taylor whispered close to Christian's ear.

"He doesn't like anybody. He views others in a different way. It has nothing to do with like or any emotion most would recognize. Nigel is very hard to explain, but he's been decent about my education." Christian slid his hand down to Taylor's to drag him away from the more populated hallways toward the back of the sanctified halls.

Taylor's heart skipped a beat the second Christian's hand slipped into his. "Yeah..." he murmured. "So... temple. Temple is good."

"Better to avoid everybody else for the time being. You haven't been formally introduced yet." Once they reached a towering set of engraved metal doors, Christian released Taylor's hand to grab the large ring at eye level. When he let it go, a resounding thud echoed around them, then an ominous creak announced the opening of the doors.

"I think I prefer your company. I'm quite fond of-" Taylor's eyes widened when he got his first look at the temple. "Holy shit."

"This is where the really old ones like to worship, or have orgies, whichever you prefer to call it."

The enormous white marble floor was easily as large as two city blocks, inlaid with distinct emerald and azure patterns. Twenty-foot statues of Roman gods and goddesses lined both sides of the room, against the walls. Metal bowls, as tall as Taylor's shoulders and blazing with fire, led the way to a staircase that stretched the entire width of the room. A large altar sat atop in solitary splendor.

Awestruck, Taylor just stared at the immense room, words utterly failing him. He walked over to one of the statues—Cupid, he realized—and touched it. The smooth stone felt cool, but Taylor swore he sensed the god's essence radiating through the marble. He stroked his fingertips along the statue's leg, then up to touch the bottom of Cupid's legendary bow.

"Any images of orgies?" Christian teased. He was closer than Taylor realized when he whispered in Taylor's ear. "It's almost like he's alive, isn't it?"

A shiver slid up Taylor's spine when he sensed a presence at the edge of his awareness. He closed his eyes. "I hear him," he murmured. He focused on the sensations and, a moment later, gasped. Oh, he saw something all right, but it wasn't an orgy. "No orgy. Just... two people."

"You're lucky. Even I can sense only faint echoes. I don't think he touches many. Most aren't looking for him when they come here." The look Christian gave Taylor held the slightest touch of envy. "Don't come here when the others are here. This place takes on a whole different atmosphere."

"No worries there." Taylor found it rather difficult to pull his attention from the statue. If he did, he'd end up facing one of the participants he'd seen in his... vision. "Do you sense one stronger than the others?"

Christian rested his hand against the smoothness of Cupid's leg, gaze glued to the god's handsome features. "I'm not sure you could call it a sense. Just more a whisper of something, but it eludes me."

Taylor wanted to tell Christian exactly what he saw, but he bit his tongue to keep quiet about it. "He..." Taylor wondered on the wisdom of saying a word, but he continued anyway. "He sees you. He knows you're here, and where you will go. It's all he will tell me."

Christian appeared momentarily shocked, but it faded to something resembling relief. "Guess maybe I wasn't crazy." He gave a self-conscious laugh. "I come here a lot, and most of the time, I sit right there at the base near his bow. Nobody else comes here at all except for worship nights."

The image lingering in Taylor's mind brought back the reading he'd done for Christian. He shot a disbelieving look at the statue's face. "You can't be serious," he muttered under his breath.

"What?"

Taylor looked at Christian, forcing his own gaze to remain on Christian's eyes and not the man's lips. "Are you really sure you want to know any of this?"

When Christian answered, he didn't sound so certain. "I probably don't want to know, do I? Maybe you should just leave it for me to figure out some day."

"Agreed." Taylor had no clue how Christian would react to knowing what he now did. "Besides, surprises are more... fun."

"Good enough for me." Christian's normal sunny smile returned, doing weird things to Taylor's insides. The only time Christian behaved so openly was when they were together in private. Any other time, Taylor had noticed, Christian was far more formal, cold, and unreadable.

"Come on," Taylor said, taking Christian's hand in his. "Show me more of the palace."

"There are the formal gardens, the not-so-formal gardens, and the ones where mortals take advantage of vampires. Any of them appeal to you?"

"Mortals take advantage of vampires?" Taylor eyed him dubiously. "Dare I ask?"

"There are a lot of mortals who are addicted to vampire bites. Diocourides makes sure even they are well treated. There's a particular garden where vampires can go if they want to be fair game." Christian shrugged with a marked lack of interest. "Not something I do, but there's nothing wrong with it."

"Don't blame you. I think we'll just stick to the formal or not-so-formal gardens."

Christian tugged on his hand. "Then let's head outside."

* * *

Diocourides sat on the top step of the dais, legs crossed, hands resting on his thighs. The others before him talked amongst themselves as he listened to the main speaker.

"I believe we can sustain an increase of five percent in our overall population, Diocourides. The real problem is deciding how many each country will receive." Ambrogio, one of his first formulas, shuffled the papers in his hands, then peered down at Dio.

"Leave the papers with Roberto. I'll study your reports later this evening and give an answer within the next two nights."

As Ambrogio stepped back, Amelia, Dio's second-in-command and eldest daughter, took his place. "Father, we've received two more staking reports: one off the Via del Traforo, the other near the Via Celio Verbenna not too far from the Arco di Constantino. The total is now five, of which three were destroyed."

Alarm rustled through the onlookers at the unwelcome news. When whispers of the words 'Holy Sons' reached him, Dio raised a hand for silence. "We will investigate all avenues. Rumors are not proof. There will be no accusations until we have positive proof of who is behind the stakings." He glanced back at his daughter. "Arrange a public session for tomorrow evening in the central court."

"I will get out the word immediately, father." She bowed to him before she turned on her heel to do his bidding.

A young man stood in the doorway and waited until he had Dio's attention. "Prince Nigel is here to see you, Diocourides."

"Come on in, Nigel. Everybody else is just leaving." That's all it took for the room to empty in rapid order.

Nigel bowed and as soon as the doors closed, giving them privacy, he sat on one of the cushioned benches near Diocourides. "I've come regarding my son, or, more importantly, his poor choice in companion."

"I know you've heard the rumors just as I have, Nigel. There is no truth to the sorcerer using any magic on Mael. You know damn well I'd know if there were."

Nigel's jaw tensed as he gritted his teeth. "It is... unseemly. Mael is a prince. He should not be gallivanting with someone known to hunt our kind. Rogues or not, Carmichael kills vampires. Others believe he is behind the were tribe poisonings, and possibly the stakings, too."

"Nigel, he was a great deal of help during the rogue crisis, but he no longer hunts. Furthermore, he has poisoned no one." Dio paused, giving Nigel a sympathetic look. "You are one of my favorite and best princes, Nigel, and there is a great deal I would do for you. However, I fail to understand what you expect me to do."

"I want Cian Carmichael out of the picture," Nigel said bluntly. "Mael's relationship with him is a stain on my family."

Dio sighed. He'd expected Nigel wouldn't give up. "You'd be best served by leaving those two alone, my old friend. They're devoted to one another. Now come, tell me, what is your opinion on the proposed five percent increase of our numbers? I have my reservations, but would like your honest input."

"If bloodlines remain intact and respected, then I am behind the idea. We've had a rash of questionable offspring of late, Aldrich being one of the worst, I wager."

"Nigel, the problem with Aldrich had nothing to do with bloodlines. He couldn't adjust to our way and paid the ultimate price. Trust your son's judgment. He's done very little wrong in the past, and you well know it." He doubted if reasoning with Nigel would work, but he had to try.

"It had everything to do with blood. Look who his father-" Nigel snapped his mouth shut.

"I'm going to overlook that, Nigel, and remind you that you're well within your rights to call an official questioning on your son. But do you really want to take it that far? Should the counsel deem him unfit, he'll be stripped of everything, and it won't reflect at all well on you."

Nigel seemed to think on it for a moment. "No," he said finally. "Not yet, at any rate."

"A wise choice. You know, you might disagree with Mael's choice, but Carmichael is an excellent companion and will make an outstanding father for Taylor. You have nothing to worry about, I assure you." Dio stood and gestured Nigel to join him. "I'm letting you head the next session since I must attend to a matter in the United States. Thought I'd warn you ahead of time instead of dropping it on you like last time."

Nigel froze mid-stride. "What did you say? About Carmichael and Taylor?"

"Carmichael will be an excellent father for Taylor. For Christian as well." One brow raised, he dared Nigel to refute the statements.

"Mael is Christian's father, and he will be Taylor's. Carmichael has absolutely no bearing on either of them."

"You're allowed your own opinion, but take care not to drive your son away." He stepped off the dais and headed out of the room.

Following on Dio's heels, Nigel said, "Mael's blood is within Christian. His blood will be within Taylor. This is not opinion, it is fact. Carmichael has no stake in Taylor's future."

"Carmichael will help train him, Nigel. Taylor will benefit a great deal from it." There was no way he could or would tell Nigel the truth. Too many hated any mixing of blood. Nigel was worse than most.

"What could Carmichael possibly teach someone fathered within my family line?"

Now he walked a fine line and knew it. He couldn't reveal too much, but he wanted Nigel to understand how important Cian's skills could be to his progeny. "He killed quite a few powerful vampires on his own. His fighting skills will serve Taylor in good stead should the boy ever have need of them. Christian would do well with lessons from him, too."

"Absolutely not." Nigel stood ramrod straight, arms crossed. "I may not have any say over Taylor's future, but Christian is living within my home."

"Stubborn old fool. You always were the worst about your family." Dio laughed and shook his head. "I'd be the last to tell you how to raise your own, but I truly believe you do a disservice to Christian in this."

"I may be stubborn, but my family is pure."

"Yes, yes, the end all and be all of vampirehood. I know, I know." He paused in front of his office door. "Just think about what I've told you, Nigel. And give some thought to the five percent notion, all right?" When he finished, he opened the door and went inside, closing the door behind him.

Chapter Nine

Apollonius went to great lengths to avoid the home he supposedly shared with Triarius and Lance. He heard the rumors, whispered here and there, about their bizarre love triangle and its rocky future, but he made certain no one knew he was back in Rome after a visit to the States. He had more important matters to attend. If his plans were to work, he needed help. He needed someone who held more power than Mael Black. As a third formula, Apollonius knew he was no match for the second formula ruler of London. But... he knew who was.

"I've come to speak to Prince Nigel. It's regarding..." Apollonius smiled at the valet. "... his son."

Nigel stepped into the foyer. "I'll take care of this, Antonio."

"Yes, your Excellency." The man bowed to Nigel before he headed down the hall.

"What about my son, Apollonius?" The prince gestured for Apollonius to join him in an office.

Confident they were alone, Apollonius bowed. "I've come to propose an alliance."

Hands behind his back, Nigel faced the portrait of himself and his oldest son hanging above the mantle of the fireplace. "An alliance for what purpose? Seems you've little favor in our hallowed halls these days."

For the briefest moment, Apollonius bristled at the reminder. He quickly brought his emotions under control, however, and regained a cold composure. "And I have heard that a particular sorcerer has become a thorn in your side, given his questionable influence over your son."

Nigel turned his head and glanced at Apollonius. "We both have our problems. If you have a solution, speak plainly. If not, you may leave now."

"London has been inundated with were creatures. It would be a shame if the tribes were to suddenly become violently ill. Rumors, as you well know, can spread like wildfire." Apollonius wandered over to one of the bookshelves and studied the titles for a moment. "If the weres suspected Black's court of the poisoning, all eyes would focus on the sorcerer and his magic. Would they not?"

"I suppose they might. Am I to take it you are behind that particular problem?"

Apollonius pulled a vial from his coat pocket and set it on Nigel's desk. "Silver Asperia. Within a few days after ingestion, many of them will fall ill, some will die. The task set before me is unimportant for now. What I need is someone who can assist me in bringing London to its knees. In return, I will set the wheels in motion to rid you of your problem. Only a sorcerer of Carmichael's means and caliber could afford such an ingredient."

"My only interest is ridding my son of an unacceptable companion. Just how much damage are you planning in London?"

"Enough to convince Diocourides to banish Carmichael, if not sign the sorcerer's death warrant outright."

"A death warrant would be preferable." Nigel turned to face Apollonius, a faint smile on his lips. There was nothing but coldness in his eyes, no hint of emotion or warmth. "What is it you want from me?"

"Assistance." Apollonius spread his arms in mock self-depreciation. "I am only a third formula. If I am to succeed in what I've been commanded to do, I need the backing of someone in a much higher position than that of a guard such as myself."

"You will have my considerable aid at your disposal, but should anything go wrong, all of the consequences will fall on you. My name will not be found. Am I understood?" Nigel returned his gaze to the portrait above him. "Deal with Carmichael, and you will find a place in the Romanorum with my help."

"It will be done, your Excellency."

Apollonius left the prince and stepped out once more into the cold night. With Nigel's aid, his next task held much more promise. Given his frequent trips to America, Apollonius knew no one would bat an eye if he vanished to London. He had a mission and intended to follow through on it. He summoned a portal and stepped through, emerging a few moments later in the shadows of a London alley. His research pointed him to a warehouse complex where one of the tribes had taken to storing their food supplies. It was time to set things into motion.

The warehouse stood in a quieter, if not somewhat run-down district. Apollonius made certain no one saw him as he approached one of the side entrances. "I've come to see your leader," he said to the two monstrous, half-shifted guards blocking his way. "I've heard of your disquiet and would like to offer my assistance in whatever way I can."

Neither man seemed much impressed. One gestured to the door behind him and said, "Follow me."

The were made his way around the half-rusted equipment and boxes strewn all over to a lit office in one far corner. Other weres were busy in the main room, storing supplies. When they reached the office, a guard opened the door, then stood to the side. Apollonius nodded his thanks and entered. The office didn't look much different from the rest of the warehouse: cluttered, full of supply boxes. Behind a ragged desk, a man sat, head bent over a binder of some sort. Apollonius cleared his throat and the man looked up.

"Who are you?"

Apollonius bowed. "My name is Apollonius. Having heard of the unrest your tribes are experiencing, I'd hoped to help, if I can."

A woman peeked over the top of a stack of boxes. "And why would you do that?"

"Peace between our species is best attained by cooperation and mutual understanding," Apollonius said. "Am I right?"

The woman narrowed her eyes, but nodded. "That is a rather surprising thing to hear, but I can't exactly argue with your logic."

Apollonius smiled. "I don't wish to intrude, but I swear that I will do whatever is necessary to establish peace, and perhaps friendship, between our kinds."

"We could always use another pair of strong arms." Stepping from behind the boxes, she motioned to the man to leave the office. "The name is Linda. I'm head of this tribe. You part of Black's court?"

"It's a pleasure," Apollonius said. "Although I have occasional contact with Prince Black, I came directly from Rome."

"I see. Well, we need help getting all the food stores ready for distribution. I know it's a menial task, but it must be done."

"Where did the food come from? It's quite a lot."

"Prince Black sent it. I'm assuming to placate the grumblings here and there, but we're not about to dismiss the offer." Linda handed him a clipboard and pen. "Just inventory everything, then let the guys in the warehouse know it's ready to be doled out to the masses."

Apollonius gave her his best smile and a slight bow. "My pleasure."

Linda left him to his work, and Apollonius surveyed the crates. Confident he wasn't in sight of anyone, he took out a syringe and the vial. The viscous concoction appeared rather harmless, but he'd seen first-hand the effects: hallucinations, lethargy, vomiting, and in some cases, death.

It would do quite nicely, he thought as he plunged the needle into the first chunk of plastic-wrapped meat.

* * *

"You summoned me, grandfather." Christian bowed, then straightened.

"Sit, boy. Relax. I only wanted to talk with you and see how things were progressing." Nigel waited until Christian sat down before continuing. "Pour yourself a glass of blood. It's a rare specialty I found. Not often I come across a specially treated bottle like this one."

Clearly intrigued, Christian poured himself a generous portion before he carefully resealed the bottle.

"Have you been able to get your father to see sense, child?" Nigel asked as he watched. It would take very little of the magical concoction to affect Christian. For the price he'd paid, it had better do what its creator had promised. His personal secretary entered the room and waited by the door. David was the epitome of discretion, and Nigel trusted the man with his life. He'd been with Nigel for more than a millennium.

"Grandfather, I don't believe there is any way to separate those two." Christian took a swallow. "This is very good. Can I afford a bottle?"

"You could afford a few, Christian, but I have a case in my cellar. I'm willing to share."

A moment later, David jumped forward to catch Christian's glass before it fell to the floor.

"It worked as fast as promised. I'm impressed. Remember to give more business to Derno."

"Yes, your Excellency. Are you positive your son is not in his rooms at the Romanorum?"

"He'll be busy for another hour or so. More than enough to do what I need you to do. This should bring Mael back to his senses. He never could resist Christian for long, not even at his angriest. Things will soon be as they should be."

David nodded, then lifted Christian's unconscious body from the chair.

* * *

It hadn't been easy ditching one of the most persistent committees in the Romanorum, but Mael had managed. He considered them to be nonsense with their antiquated ideas. To Mael, moving with the future was the only way to insure their survival and cohabitation with mortals. With a quiet sigh, he basked in the quiet as he opened his bedroom door. It had been kind of Diocourides to house them in his personal section. It kept everybody else at bay when Mael wanted a few moments to himself.

The first thing to hit him was an odd scent in the room. He closed the door and looked around. Something had triggered a response from him to breathe, and he had no idea what it was. A strong aroma of arousal flooded his senses, confusing him further. A low groan from the direction of the bed got his attention. He walked to it, drew back the bed curtains, and froze in surprise. The sight of Christian in the bed, minus his clothes, floored Mael. What the hell was the boy doing?

A strong permeation aroused Mael to an almost unbearable level, yet he fought against the insistent urge rising in him. The sheer strength of whatever had been used was a testament to its creator's power, and it took most of Mael concentration to ignore it. Christian's eyes fluttered open, then shut again. Just as Mael reached out, he realized his son wasn't fully conscious. He ran a hand just above Christian's body, and it helped his senses pick up the smallest magical trace. A deep anger replaced his first reactions.

This wasn't Christian's doing. The boy wouldn't put himself in Mael's bed in an unconscious state. There was only one other candidate who would dare do something this stupid. It had to be his father's interference. No doubt Nigel hoped

Mael would see Christian and be aroused enough to fuck him without thought. If not, the magical spell would make it impossible for Mael to control himself. If anything, it had the opposite effect. Christian's vulnerability brought out a strong protective instinct in Mael that Nigel apparently didn't consider.

The man had no right to drag Christian into this. Mael carefully pulled the covers from beneath Christian, covering him. A soft touch to his cheek and the use of Mael's power helped burn the magic from Christian's system to leave him in a natural sleep. Then Mael straightened and left his room. This nonsense was uncalled for. He strode down the hall, intent on a few words with his father.

* * *

Cian closed the book he'd been reading and rubbed his eyes. As an angel, he honestly didn't need sleep—unless Mael made sure of it—but here lately, they both ended up on the receiving end of more stress than usual. He realized he missed London greatly. He got up and placed the book back on its shelf before leaving the office. Just as he stepped out into the hallway, he caught a glimpse of Mael going the other direction. The prince seemed intent, so Cian let him be for now.

Just before he got to their bedroom door, however, it opened once more. Cian watched, utterly dumbstruck, as Christian—a very naked Christian—walked out. Of their bedroom. After Mael had left. Stunned, Cian couldn't speak. Christian didn't even seem to notice him as the young man went across the hall and disappeared into his own room.

It took several seconds before Cian found the power to even move. Surely Christian and Mael hadn't... Cian shook his head. "No. Mael wouldn't do that." As he stepped into their private sanctuary away from the insanity of the Romanorum, Cian fought back the tiny voice in his head that wanted to argue.

* * *

"No need to announce me, David. My father won't be surprised to see me." Mael pushed past the protesting man, but before he got a step further, Nigel came out of one of the rooms. "I believe we have something to discuss, father."

Nigel motioned David to leave them.

"If your Excellency needs me, I won't be far away." He bowed to Nigel, then Mael.

"Don't worry, David, I won't harm him, even if he deserves it." While his father was more powerful, Mael could make Nigel damn sorry for crossing him.

"It wouldn't be that easy, child."

"Don't bet on it, old man," Mael growled at him. "Don't try to use my son against me, Nigel. He's done nothing to deserve treatment like that from you."

"Christian makes his own choices." A shrug followed the noncommittal comment.

"I found him in my bed, unconscious. I'm damn sure he didn't put himself there," Mael snapped, his voice rising with his temper.

"I didn't put him there if that's what you are getting at." The cool, unemotional shell Nigel had perfected was on full display. "So don't accuse me of it."

"Damn it, Nigel. You're responsible for it. Keep it up, and I'll drag Diocourides into this if I have to. Don't think I won't come after you myself. Leave my son out of this." He didn't bother to restrain his anger. His father needed a good does of reality, and Mael wouldn't hesitate to give it to him. Mael turned away from Nigel in disgust, then paused. "In fact, you really don't need to worry about the boy at all. I want him back with me." With that parting shot, Mael left his father's residence.

Chapter Ten

"I heard he's behind the poisonings in London."

"Why would he do that?"

"He's a sorcerer. He has the power to do it."

Cian halted outside a half-open door to one of the studies. Inside, a group of vampires stood talking and sipping wine or blood, some of them preferring to take their nourishment from the source. The conversation topic, however, worried him.

"He's the prince's consort," one of the vampires said. "Do you really think he'd start trouble like that?"

"Like I said, he knows magic. From what I hear from a few friends in London, Carmichael is really good at what he does." A few seconds later, the speaker's voice dropped conspiratorially. "I even heard he bewitched the prince."

"No..."

"Think about it," another one said. "A sorcerer with unknown powers in a city ripe for the taking. All he has to do is cast a spell, and the prince and everyone else is under his command."

Eyes narrowing, Cian scowled. Where on earth did they come up with this stuff? He'd been blamed for quite a few instances of spellbound madness, though he'd never done anything like it.

"Do you really think he would do something like that, though? I mean, sure, he's powerful, but why would he poison the were tribes?"

"Boredom? I'd bet he's behind the stakings, too."

Several of them laughed. Cian didn't. Leaving the group to their ridiculous gossip, he headed for Mael's office. The door sat ajar, Mael behind the desk and reading over a stack of papers. Cian walked in and shut the door behind him.

Mael glanced up. "You look... unhappy."

"To say the least," Cian said. He sat down in one of the chairs and let his head fall backward, eyes closing. "Apparently I'm behind the were problems back home."

"What?" Mael laughed. "Where the hell did you get that idea?"

"Oh, hearsay." Cian lifted his head and fixed Mael with what he figured was a rather disgruntled gaze. "There are rumors pegging me as the culprit."

"What are they saying?"

"That I poisoned the were tribes out of boredom. Oh, and that I obviously bewitched you."

Mael smirked. "I can't exactly argue with that last bit, though I don't think it's quite like the idiots out there are saying."

"Mael," Cian sighed. "Out of all the things going on right now, why can't they all find something more productive to focus on?"

"Because you're you."

One eyebrow rose. "Very funny."

"I'm serious." Mael got up and walked around the desk. He flicked the lock on the door and knelt down in front of Cian. Hands on Cian's thighs, the prince fixed him with a stare somewhere between playful and lascivious. "You're gorgeous. You're powerful. You possess magic they don't."

"You're trying to distract me," Cian muttered, watching as the prince's hands inched up his legs.

"Is it working?"

Cian swallowed as Mael's fingers neared the junction where thigh met groin. He shifted in the chair, growing hard despite his earlier grumbling. "It might be..."

Mael grinned and popped the button Cian's leather pants. "Door's locked. I'm not due to see Dio for about an hour."

Whatever Cian wanted to say disappeared entirely the moment the prince's long fingers curled around his length. Cian moaned softly, hips lifting. Mael winked, then bent down and swiped his tongue up Cian's shaft.

"Mael."

"Fuck, you taste good," the prince murmured. He sucked Cian down, slow and easy.

Cian gasped and threaded his fingers in the silky black hair spilling over his lap. He held it back so he could see his lover's lips wrapped tight around his prick. Mael sucked and stroked, every slick slide of those fingers and that wickedly talented tongue had Cian coming before he expected it. Groaning, he thrust his cock down Mael's throat and shuddered. Mael's growl vibrated through him, then the prince licked him clean.

Panting, Cian stared down at the man before him. "What was I bitching about?"

Mael chuckled and tucked him back into his pants. "Something about how long it's been since you've had my cock in your ass."

Cian squirmed slightly. "So why are we talking?"

* * *

Cornelius had warned Mael he would be showing up with Linda Ellsworth as soon as they could get away from London. So Mael wasn't surprised when they both exited a portal of darkness near his desk. How his magician had talked the were leader into traveling via the shadows was beyond Mael. He thanked the gods that they'd waited, though. If they'd arrived just a few hours ago, it probably would've scarred the poor woman for life. When he gestured for them to sit, they both took a chair in front of his desk. Cornelius started in right away.

"We've got a serious problem, Mael. The food supplies we had in the warehouse were poisoned."

"Three have already died, and ten are hospitalized. We need to find out what the hell is going on, Mael." Linda's tone rose with her anger. "I'm not sure how much longer the tribes will stay under my leadership. Many are questioning my decision to accept your help.

"I don't know who is behind this, Linda, but I can assure you, it's not me. I have nothing to gain from any were death, and too much trouble to gain from it."

"I know or I wouldn't be here now. I don't hold you responsible, but I'll quickly be a minority if there's anymore trouble."

"I've already tested about half of the supplies and destroyed all the tainted food.," Cornelius said. "We'll use what's in the palace stores if we run out before I can test the rest. I'll also test anything we get coming in for the weres."

It sounded like his mage had things well in hand. His confidence in Cornelius had always been well placed. "Include as many weres in the testing as you can. Hopefully, they'll spread the word about what we're doing and how safe the food is."

"I will take care of it, Mael."

Mael glanced at Linda and asked without pause, "If you witness a Sphere of Truth, do you think it will convince others?"

Surprised, she frowned. "I hope it won't be necessary, but we may have to use one if we can't get this under control."

"Keep it in mind if it does become necessary. I will willingly submit to one." It would be painful as hell, but it might be the only proof the weres would believe. "I need to leave for the Vatican. Keep me in the loop on this, both of you. None of us can afford any more poisonings." Mael stood and walked out from behind his desk.

The other two got up as well and disappeared through another portal. With the new poisonings and reports of vampire stakings in Rome, Mael couldn't contain his increasing worry. He had an appointment with the Vatican Secretary of State to discuss the stakings. The knock at the door told him the limousine driver had arrived to take him to visit Cardinal Berdette.

During the drive to the Vatican, Mael pondered the current problems. He had a bad feeling they were all tied to the initial warning Diocourides had received from Sagan. Too much was happening at once to be otherwise. The Romanorum had its far share of problems, but the poisonings and stakings were all too coincidental. Though some blamed the Holy Sons for the stakings, Mael thought they might be from the same hand as the poisonings. This meeting with Cardinal Berdette would confirm what Mael already believed to be true: the Church wasn't behind the stakings.

Just in case, Mael tried to keep his thoughts from becoming too partial, one way or the other. He wanted the truth, not what he might think was the truth. When the car stopped, the driver got out and opened the door for Mael.

An elderly man waited on the steps for Mael to join him. "Welcome, Prince Mael. I am Father MacKenzie, Cardinal Berdette's secretary. His Eminence is in his private library. I will take you to him."

Mael bowed his head in polite respect. "Thank you, Father MacKenzie."

In silence, they walked up the steps and into the building. This wasn't Mael first visit. He'd visited many times over the years. The only things that really changed were the people who worked there. He stopped when the priest did and waited while Father MacKenzie knocked on the door, then opened it.

"Your Eminence, Prince Mael has arrived."

A deep, gravelly voice answered, "Show him in."

The priest gestured for Mael to enter, then turned away. Mael closed the door behind him.

"Your Eminence, thank you for seeing me." Mael bowed and kissed the Cardinal's ring.

"Prince Black, it's a pleasure to see you even if the topic of our conversation is not to be so pleasant. Please sit."

"I realize it is a sensitive subject to the Church, Cardinal Berdette, but we had two more vampires staked in the last week. One was destroyed by the sun. Her killer remained close enough to remove the stake right before the rays of sun reached her. Early morning passerby were alerted by the woman's screams as she burned. The other also had his heart removed."

Cardinal Berdette winced. "Horrible. I wish I had answers for you, but I don't. I can assure you, however, that none of this is, in any way, connected with the Church."

"Has his Holiness given his permission for me to view the last of the Holy Sons files? The Romanorum needs some kind of proof we can give to our members. We've tried to stop the rumors, but it's near impossible as I'm sure you're aware." Without some access to those records, rumors of the Holy Sons would continue and Mael knew it. So did the Pope and Cardinal.

"Absolutely." The Cardinal stood and retrieved a rather large stack of folders. He set them on the desk in front of Mael. "You know we will help in whatever way we can, Prince Black, but the majority of Holy Sons' documents will remain under lock and key."

"I promised his Holiness I would only use the files relevant to the forced disbandment. He can rely on both my discretion and Diocourides." Mael managed to maintain a genial tone. It was well known the Church had been an active supporter of the Holy Sons; they just chose to ignore the reality of their past involvement. "I'll review the copies and make sure they are a match for the originals."

"Take your time," the Cardinal said. Hands folded in front of him on the desk, he watched Mael in silence before speaking again. "I know the Church has its... sordid past with your people, but we've tried to move beyond it. A lot of the older ones here have simply chosen to ignore that such a time even existed."

"We are doing our best as well, your Eminence. I know Diocourides appreciates his Holiness' assistance, and the help you've given to quell the nonsense of the rumors. It is imperative to discover who is behind the stakings."

The door opened behind him, and Father MacKenzie came in. "Please follow me, Prince Mael. I'll take you to one of the private rooms for you to peruse the files."

"Thank you, your Eminence." Before Mael picked up the folders, he stood, bowed once again to the Cardinal, and kissed his ring.

Chapter Eleven

"Master Carmichael?"

Cian turned to the woman beside him and smiled. "Please, call me Cian," he said, offering his hand. She blushed and gave it a timid shake. "What can I do for you?"

"I hope I'm not being too forward, but I heard some others talking. They said you're a sorcerer. Is that true?"

Although he'd not done anything overtly magical since they'd arrived in Rome, Cian wasn't entirely surprised to find out the rumors continued beyond the usual accusations. "I am."

She chewed on her lower lip and Cian thought she was actually quite pretty. "Can you... I mean, do you..."

"How about we continue this discussion somewhere more private?" Cian gestured toward one of the little-used offices lining the corridor, just a few doors down from Mael's temporary study. He closed the door behind them. "What can I do for you?"

The young woman sat in one of the chairs. "I'm just a mortal staff member, but... there's someone I like. A vampire. I think he likes me, too, but I'm too nervous."

One eyebrow lifting, Cian eyed her, a bit wary. "If what you need is something along the lines of a love potion, then I'm afraid I can't do that."

"Oh, no!" She actually looked shocked. "I would never want anyone to fall in love with me thanks to a spell or a potion. I just... I need a boost in my..." She blushed. "... sex appeal."

Smiling, Cian crouched in front of her. "I understand. While I personally think you're beautiful, everyone needs a bit of a perk to their self-esteem."

"But... don't you like guys?"

Cian laughed. "Yes, I do. Specifically one, but even Prince Black isn't beyond admiring beauty when he sees it. I will create something for you."

"Thank you." She stood as Cian did. "You're a lot nicer than most of the others here."

"It's in my nature," Cian said. He opened the door, bowed, and followed her out into the hall. "Come see me in a few days."

With a smile and a slight bow of her own, she left. Cian turned in the direction of Mael's study, his original destination, when someone else stopped him. This woman, however, almost leered at him, a cold but appreciative gaze sweeping over Cian.

"Cate's been after Andrew for a while," the vampire said. "I, however, have more important matters."

Cian crossed his arms, not at all liking where this particular conversation was headed. "And that would be?"

The female vampire did nothing to mask the venom in her voice. "My ex-lover has been flaunting his newest conquest all over town. I want the little tramp he's toying with to learn she doesn't stand a chance."

"In other words, you want revenge."

"Yes. Nothing to maim or kill, of course, but enough to make the whore wish she'd never crossed a vampire's path."

Cian gritted his teeth and silently counted to ten. "No."

"What?" The woman looked as if she'd never had anyone deny her, though her current predicament said otherwise. "What do you mean, no?"

"I mean I am not going to help you torment someone just because you're jealous."

"But I'm a vampire!"

"You..." Cian said, voice dropping low enough for only her ears, "are a spurned lover with a chip on your shoulder."

The woman gaped like a fish. "How-how dare you! I'll report you to the prince!"

Cian chuckled and turned away, giving her a last glance over one shoulder. "Believe me, Prince Black has heard much worse in regard to me."

Purposely ignoring her, Cian prayed no one else stopped him. When he stopped in front of Mael's office, he sighed in relief. Beyond this door, he could at least enjoy a moment of peace. Schooling his mood into something calmer, he opened the door.

"Mael, I swear, if anyone else..." Cian froze, words stuck in his throat.

A soft growl came from Christian at the interruption, but he didn't stop his feeding. Mael opened his eyes and mouthed to Cian, "One minute."

What smile there had been fell within seconds. Cian forced his gaze away from the sight of Christian straddling Mael. He shut the door none-too-gently, then headed straight for the bedroom. It took every ounce of effort he had to maintain some semblance of civility.

"When you're done, feel free to join me.

It took quite a bit longer than a minute before Cian heard the cessation of periodic growls from Mael's son. The soft murmur of Mael's voice reached him, but the words were indistinguishable. A laugh sounded from Christian, followed by Mael's.

The sound felt like a dozen knives slicing through Cian. He slammed the bedroom door hard enough to rattle everything in the room. The image burned into his brain, he jerked open the balcony doors and, for a brief moment, considered giving away his true form if it meant escaping what he'd seen. Maybe he'd been wrong to dismiss Christian leaving Mael's room naked days ago. Just the thought of what else he'd missed fueled his anger.

It wasn't long after that the door opened and Mael entered, alone. "What's wrong?"

Cian spun around, wings unfurling in fury, despite the open doors behind him. "What's wrong?" he shouted. Entire body thrumming, he began pacing, jealousy overtaking everything else. "What the fuck else have you two been doing when I'm gone?"

"Do you mean me and my son?"

Cian stalked closer to Mael, hissing under his breath. "Is there anyone else I should be 'watching my back' for, your Highness?"

"Cian, I was feeding Christian, nothing more." Mael laid his hand on Cian's arm.

Cian's gaze shifted from Mael's face to his arm, then back again. "Is that why he might as well have been riding your cock?"

Mael stiffened before closing the balcony doors. All they needed was someone seeing Cian's wings. When he turned back to the angel, the dark aura of his true nature took full hold of him. "Closeness is a part of feeding *my child*, Cian. I begrudge neither my blood nor the physical touch he requires. I never will. I was not fucking him. Christian is my son. The only blood not from a bottle he gets is from me. Nigel won't feed him, and Christian refuses to feed from anyone not of our family. He needs me. Not just when it's convenient for you or me, and you need to understand that."

Cian jerked his arm out of Mael's grasp, eyes turning bright silver. His wings curled downward around him, reminiscent of their battle with Memnet's demon. Something wasn't right. From the waves of ever increasing rage, Mael realized he wasn't getting through to Cian. At that point, he decided to try one last resort. He called out to Taylor in his mind. The boy and Cian shared a bond that Mael prayed would work to diffuse the situation.

"I need you. Can you attend to me at once?"

Mael opened a portal and Taylor stepped through. The boy took one look at Cian and his expression went from curious to concern.

"What happened? Mael, what's going on?"

"Now, tell me, my angel, is there anything you wouldn't do for him," Mael said, pointing to Taylor. Then Mael turned to the young man, all coldness gone at once as he smiled. "Just a disagreement about what a father does for his child."

Realization dawned on Taylor's face. "He saw Christian feeding, didn't he?" It seemed to galvanize Taylor into action. Ignoring Mael, he turned his attention solely to Cian. "I know you're in there," he whispered.

After a few seconds, the angel's glare fixed on Taylor. Something about Cian seemed... otherworldly, far more than the angel's usual presence. It was as if Cian didn't even see them at all. Hell, it didn't seem like Cian. Mael stayed back, watching. If feeding his son brought this out in Cian, Mael wasn't at all sure what to make of it. Could Cian hurt them? He banished the thought as soon as he'd had it.

"Cian." Taylor narrowed his gaze, as if someone had whispered in his head. "Surael." A flicker of recognition shone in the angel's eyes. "Release him, Surael. Cian wouldn't want this."

The use of Cian's true name surprised Mael, especially since no one should know the name, save for himself and Michael. When Taylor spoke again, the mortal's voice sounded thunderous.

"Surael, I *command* you to release him!"

Within a few seconds of the order, the air seemed to leave Cian's body and he dropped to his knees. His wings faded from sight and he shuddered, gasping for breath. Taylor knelt down and brushed golden hair from the angel's sweat-slick forehead.

"Hey, Father, is something..." Christian entered and closed the door behind him, his words trailing off as he took in the scene.

"What have I done?" Cian whispered, though his voice sounded raw, hoarse.

"You..." Taylor looked at Mael, Christian, and back to Cian. "You threatened Mael," he said. "Christian is his son, and Mael will do anything for him. Just like you would for me."

Cian finally met Mael's gaze, his blue-gray eyes full of sorrow and regret. "Please... forgive me, my prince."

"I would forgive you anything, my angel. Just understand: he is my child. That's all I ask."

"I felt something wrong. What's going on?" Christian asked.

Taylor left Cian's side and joined Christian. "I'll tell you later."

Cian stood slowly, though he looked, for a moment, like he was dizzy. "Mael. I... I need some time." Before anyone could say a word, a portal opened beside him. "I love you. I will return soon." Then he stepped through, the portal closing behind him.

Mael held out his hand to Taylor, who looked deeply troubled. "Would you prefer to talk to me or Christian?"

"Should I leave or something?" With a frown, Christian stepped back toward the door.

"No." Taylor grabbed Christian's hand, holding tight. "Please. Don't go."

Mael nodded to Christian. "We'll talk later. I need to head to the main court." He disappeared into the shadows, leaving the two of them alone.

"Cian saw you feeding." Taylor stared at Christian's hand in his for a moment. "He's the jealous type, to put it mildly. But... when they started arguing, something happened, I think." He raked his free hand through his hair. "It's like he has a split personality. There's Cian—the guy we know, the guy Mael adores and who adores Mael. Then there's... this other side of him. It's the side that only comes out in battle, I think. It takes over, and, for lack of a better term, imprisons Cian."

"You said he threatened my father. Because I was feeding?" Christian looked like he didn't know how to take that or even how he felt about it.

"Well... he did, and he didn't. Cian didn't like seeing you feeding, or the way you were doing it. How *were* you doing it, anyway?"

"Just like I always do. Mael is the only one I feed from. My grandfather refuses to let me, and the only other option is a bottle. So I make do. It's a lot better from my father." There was a pained wistfulness to Christian's voice. "I miss the closeness sometimes more than the blood. It just feels safe to be in his arms."

Taylor wanted to beg for the chance to be in Mael's shoes, but he knew better. "I wish..." He shook his head and smiled a little, thinking better of it. "It's okay. Cian would give his life for you if it came down to it. He would never harm anyone—especially someone Mael loves—out of anger."

"I'm not sure anybody would understand." Christian shrugged. "A lot of times, it's about position when someone is as high as Mael. You see it often around here."

"Mael loves you. Cian loves you, too, whether you believe it or not. And they aren't the only ones—others do, too. Sometimes, it's not about understanding, so much as it is accepting."

"Taylor." Christian gave him a serious look. "The only one I have is Nigel. It's been that way for a long time. I take Mael when I can get him. You haven't been around here for that long. You'll figure it out sooner or later."

Taylor felt an overwhelming need to throttle the young man beside him. Christian could be just as stubborn as Mael and Cian at times. "I wish you could stay here, with us."

"As much as I want to, it's hard to stay with Mael. My place is in Rome, with Nigel. I'll return to it sooner or later. It should probably be sooner rather than later, to be honest." Christian finally released Taylor's hand and sat on the edge of the bed. "Things are kind of hard to explain."

Taylor crouched in front of him, looking up into Christian's eyes. "What do I have to do? I wish you would open up to me."

"About what?"

"You've told me that you belong in Rome with Nigel, but you've never said why. Mael is your father. Why aren't you here with him?"

"Oh, that." Christian frowned, expression thoughtful. "Mael has a possessive streak a mile wide. We used to bash heads too much. I left at one point, and Nigel took me in. He's the one who's taken care of my studies. He's been quite strict about it."

"I'm beginning to think I'm the only one in this family with a level head," Taylor muttered.

Christian laughed. "You are. I dearly love my father, but we don't always get along so well."

Taylor smiled. "You should laugh more often. I could listen to it all day."

"Flattery around here gets you everywhere."

"What would it get from you?"

"Not as much as it would from others." With another laugh, Christian stood. "I think we should rescue Mael from the court ass-kissers. You with me?"

"Always."

Chapter Twelve

"You always were hot-headed."

Cian knelt at the foot of the dais, head bowed. "I never meant to hurt him like that. What have I done?"

Michael stepped down and tilted Cian's head up. "You chose to remain with him, Surael. In doing so, you accepted him, as he accepted you."

"I know."

"Mael Black, vampire or not, is human. You were created with the capacity to learn, but it is not an easy path. Humans are far more complex than we are, and they are more delicate." Michael released him and returned to the chair on the dais. "Remember that, and you will be fine."

Cian studied the archangel for a moment before speaking. "How did Taylor know my name?"

"We felt the need to gift him with the knowledge."

"We?"

"My brothers and I," Michael said. "You are a trusted friend, and a talented general, but you can still fall prey to the same dangers as humans. Love is admirable, even encouraged. You know this."

Cian bowed his head, this time in shame. He knew what was coming.

"But jealousy... it is a sin, Surael. My brothers and I saw it brewing within you, so we sent Taylor Reed the knowledge he needed to ensure you maintain control."

It made sense. Taylor had known Cian's true nature the moment they met, yet the young man had no idea how he knew. Now Cian did.

* * *

Cian didn't know what to expect upon his return. It hadn't been long to him, but Michael's palace held no concept of time. In truth, he'd been gone for two days. The thought of facing Mael after everything that had happened made him queasy. He'd never lost control like that before, and the knowledge that Mael had seen it only made him feel worse.

"I'm so sorry," he whispered to the empty room as he tried to gather his courage to even face his lover.

The door opened and Mael's voice drifted in. "No, that's not necessary, Christian. You and Taylor can take a bit of time off. I'm sure the court will hold up under your absence." Christian's laugh sounded, then became a murmur, the words too low to hear. "Later, child."

"I owe you—and Christian—an apology."

The prince stilled for a brief moment, the door closing quietly behind him. "I wasn't sure when you'd return."

Cian stood and started for Mael, but stopped. He had no idea what sort of reception he would get. "I learned a lot in my absence. About myself, but also about those around me."

"All I ask is you control whatever anger you feel over what I do for my son. You have a right to feel what you want, just realize when it comes to Christian; you'll have to control it." Mael walked toward him, holding out his hand. "Can you understand?"

"I do." Cian took Mael's hand and held it tight. "I'm not human, Mael. There are things I still have to learn."

"It's a part of you I realize I know nothing about. I wasn't sure what to do." Mael settled on the bed next to Cian, fingers tightening.

"Surael is... the warrior, created for a single purpose. When that part of me takes over, I lose sight of everything else. It's like having two spirits in one body. Surael uses the anger and jealousy to fuel what he feels to be a righteous fight. If it hadn't been for Taylor..."

"Are you capable of harming one of us, Cian?"

"No!" Cian shook his head vehemently. "I can't harm a living being in anger. Do I have the power to do so? Possibly. Can I, would I? No. The only time I would ever harm anyone is in defense. I gave up my hunting abilities, Mael."

"Is there any reason you never told me?"

"Honestly? I didn't want to worry you. I can't die a permanent death—you know that. But I gave up the ability to hunt rogues in order to return to you."

"This is all a bit much for me to take in," Mael said. "I'm just glad you've returned and things are settled between us. It's not been a fun couple of nights."

Cian slipped the fingers of his free hand through Mael's hair and eased the prince toward him. "I love you. No matter what happens, that will never change, Mael."

Mael silenced him with a hungry kiss.

* * *

"Cian?"

Cian looked up and smiled. "Come in."

Taylor slipped into the office and shut the door, hoping they'd have some time alone for a bit. "Christian said you were back. Can we talk?"

"Of course."

Taylor sat down in one of the plush leather chairs. Cian shifted in his own chair until they faced one another. "I'm not supposed to know your real name, am I?"

Cian looked as if he was going to say something, then seemed to change his mind. "In any other circumstance, no. In fact, not even my own brother knows that name. Before you, the only ones who did were Mael and Michael."

"Michael?"

Cian set the book he'd been reading to the side and leaned forward, forearms resting on his legs, hands clasped. "How much do you know about angels, Taylor?"

"Uh, not much, really. I've read about them, but that's about it."

"There is a hierarchy, extensive and practically unending. However, at the top are the archangels: Michael, Gabriel, Raphael, and Uriel. Michael is the leader, while the other three are his brothers. The rest of us fall under Michael's command in varying duties and strengths. He is our prince."

"Oh." Taylor blinked. "Wow. Okay... so where do you fit in?"

"I am one of Michael's generals, but only by my true name. He doesn't use that name unless he is issuing a command."

"Is that where you went? To see him?"

"Michael is a dear friend and my mentor. He is also the one to whom I answer when I have... erred."

"You mean sinned, don't you?"

His gaze lowering to his clasped hands, Cian sighed. "Yes. I am not human—I never was—but I possess the same faults and emotions. Jealousy is one of those."

"Mael loves you."

"I know. And I love him with every ounce of my soul. It's why I lost control when I walked in on them. Surael exists for the sole purpose of war. When I let my emotions overwhelm me, it's like I've opened the door for Surael to take over."

"Damn. That has to suck."

Cian laughed. "It can, yes."

"But it doesn't explain how I know your real name."

"Michael and his brothers felt the jealousy within me. With Mael too close to the situation, they needed someone I trust and love to hold the knowledge, should it be needed."

"So they sent it to me?"

"Yes. It's how you knew what I was before I ever opened my mouth upon our first meeting."

"That explains things," Taylor muttered. "What does it feel like to know someone has that kind of... power?"

"Humbling."

* * *

Rage, along with an unsettled feeling, boiled in Christian. Was he or was he not Mael's son? For the majority of his life, he'd had certain expectations of his father. They'd never changed in all these years. As Mael's son, he was entitled to unlimited access to his father for whatever he might need. It had always been that way. Mael had never denied him anything.

It wasn't like Mael had denied him this time either, but Christian had sensed his father was at the very edge of his limits. Something was pushing Mael to shield himself. Christian threw himself on the bed and stared out the huge double doors leading to an enclosed garden.

Nigel knew he'd returned a week ago, but had yet to summon him. There was no one else for him to talk to but his grandfather. He'd had more than enough time to contemplate everything and what it meant.

Christian realized it had to do with him feeding from Mael. While he understood there would be no sexual relationship between them, was it to include feeding as well? He'd sensed Mael's reluctance to push Cian, but he could also feel Mael didn't want to deny him. It had put Mael in enough of a quandary that Christian had decided to play least in sight.

He hadn't spoken to Nigel since the man had drugged him and put him in Mael's bed. The moment he'd woken up, he'd realized exactly who was behind it and why, but it wouldn't have done any good to say anything to Nigel. At the time, part of him had been disappointed the ploy hadn't work.

Never in his existence had he questioned his place with Mael. It had always been understood, even through the times they didn't get along well. Nigel had become the buffer between the two of them at their worst, and Mael had been in the background until needed. Now things had changed, and Christian had no clue how to adapt or what to make of it. Cian took precedence with Mael, which, to a degree, Christian understood and accepted. However, with the feeding incident, things weren't okay anymore. Cian might have calmed, but

Christian wasn't sure the angel would stay calm if he walked into the same situation again.

A sip of the bottled blood in his hand only reinforced Christian's discontent. He usually didn't mind it, but he looked forward to the taste of Mael's blood whenever he could get it. He'd been holed up at his grandfather's stronghold for almost a week, and it was all he wanted. The thought of Mael no longer there for him disturbed Christian more than he cared to admit.

"Attend to me in fifteen minutes. My study.

Christian jumped off the bed to get ready. There was a knock at the door and a second later, his valet, Simon, entered. In silence, Simon took the bottle from Christian, set it down, then opened the wardrobe to choose Christian's outfit.

With quick efficiency, Simon had him dressed and his hair coiffed in less than the allotted time. All Christian had to do was stand still and move at the appropriate moment. Before the bell sounded the half hour, Christian stood at the door of his grandfather's study

One of the servants opened the door for him and Christian went inside. He paused in front of Nigel, who was relaxing with a glass of brandy in his favorite chair, and bowed in the courtly fashion Nigel preferred.

"Good evening, grandfather."

"You've been moping about for the last five days. What is your problem?"

Leave it to Nigel to get to the heart of everything. Christian sat in the chair beside him, then accepted the glass Nigel handed over. As best he could, Christian described the situation in between sips of the brandy.

His expression impassive, Nigel gave away none of what he thought or felt. The neutral features were something Christian was used to. Nigel rarely showed any emotion at all. Silence stretched between them as Nigel poured himself another drink, then offered more to Christian.

"The sorcerer is not family, nor will he ever be. Though Mael may have forgotten his duty to his blood, he will not have forgotten his duty to you. The boy was always obsessed with you in his own way. Made it damn hard for you to stay with him, didn't it?"

Christian chuckled. Mael had been more than obsessed and jealous beyond reason. In the beginning, it hadn't bothered him, but after a time, it got old. "I hadn't thought of that."

"He is your father. Not even that *creature* Mael has in his bed can change that. I have little doubt the sorcerer would prefer you weren't around, but I suggest you don't give him what he wants. Watch yourself. Who knows what tricks such a sly wizard could use to get rid of you."

None of what his grandfather said had occurred to Christian. Could it be true? Cian had no use for him, but would the man try to get rid of him? "I'll be careful, grandfather."

"When all else is done, you had better remember your duty if Mael has indeed forgotten his. There will be no shame on the line of my blood. I'll not tolerate it." There was no emotion or anger in Nigel's statements, just a recitation of cold, hard facts. "I've been hearing more about Taylor. While I will be more than happy to receive another of Mael's children, this one had better not be meant as your replacement, thus permanently saddling me with you." A shrewd look flickered in Nigel's eyes as he studied Christian for a long moment. "You had best go back to Mael and not leave him alone with that creature. Now leave me."

His grandfather had given Christian way too much to think about. It was entirely logical that Cian wouldn't want Christian around. Why would he? But to the extent he would do harm? Would Cian do that?

Christian doubted there was room for him in Cian's life, especially since Taylor was meant to be Cian's son. A replacement? Christian felt no resentment toward Taylor. If anything, he liked the guy, more than he should. However, it could be possible Taylor would replace him.

After he stood, he bowed once again to Nigel and left the study. As Nigel had suggested, it was time to return to his father. He gathered the shadows around him and centered himself to his father's presence.

No more than a few seconds later, he stepped from the darkness and stood next to Mael. The prince smiled as Christian made himself comfortable on the arm of Mael's chair. Deep down, Christian needed to know Mael still cared about him. Mael had said the words many times, but nothing else was the same.

"You've been gone too long, child." Mael patted the hand resting on his shoulder. "I was wondering when you would return."

"You know how grandfather can be with his formalities." Christian looked between Mael and Taylor, flashing both of them a smile.

"That bad, huh?" Taylor laughed. "So what could possibly keep you so busy as to disappear from this lovely... clusterfuck?"

"Nigel has a fondness for the stiffest, longest formal parties and dinners in the history of the Romanorum."

"You've dodged the ones we had here." There was laughter in Mael's voice. "Though I will admit Nigel can surpass many for long and boring."

Taylor shuddered. "I don't want to even begin to imagine. How do you survive those things?"

"You'll get dragged to them sooner or later, Taylor." Christian smirked at him. "A new..." He paused over which exact word to use. "... friend can help. In fact, I should bring him to the next function Dio throws."

Christian glanced at Mael. One brow rose into Mael's hair line, the prince's expression no longer amused, but haughty. Ah, there it was. Christian saw it in the flicker in Mael's dark eyes. His father wasn't pleased at all. Things hadn't changed as much as he'd thought they had. Something in him relaxed, far happier than he'd been earlier.

Taylor, on the other hand, looked as if someone had punched him in the gut. "Friend... ?" he asked, voice quieter than usual, and his face paler.

Not wanting to push things with Mael, Christian shrugged and muttered, "Nobody important. Wouldn't want to bore my friends to death anyway."

"It probably wouldn't be a very good idea to bring any of your friends to a Romanorum function, child."

Taylor sank further into his chair and stared into the glass in his hand. "I miss London," he mused quietly.

"I won't. I promise, father." Christian leaned over to press a light kiss to Mael's cheek. His smile was sunny when he turned to Taylor. "Why go back there?"

Mael cast a concerned look in Taylor's direction as if he sensed something amiss. "Perhaps you and Christian should have an evening out on the town."

"Yeah, we could go to this new place I've heard about. We could get some dancing in."

"Sure. Sounds good to me." Taylor set his glass down and stood. He shoved his hands into his pockets, but seemed to look everywhere except at Christian. "After you."

Christian hopped up from his perch, in a much better mood now. "We'll have to use one of the cars since I've never been there by shadow. You can drive. You can change your clothes while I find a set of car keys, if you want."

"Will do. I'll meet you out front," Taylor said before leaving the office.

In the end, it took them more than a half hour to leave the palazzo and arrive at the club. The club was packed wall to wall with a variety of living and non-living, most dressed to excess. Christian grabbed Taylor's arm and dragged him toward the bar.

"Best to enjoy the fact you can get drunk while you can. I'll be the designated driver."

Taylor laughed. "Believe me, I will." Being around Christian made things seem less dire and stressful. He tried not to think about Christian's mention of a 'friend', and instead focused on enjoying the time he could steal. They reached the bar and one of the bartenders looked Taylor up and down, a slow grin spreading across the man's face.

"What can I get for you gentlemen," the man asked, though he seemed more interested in Taylor than anything else.

"Rum and Coke to start with," Taylor said. The bartender nodded and mixed it up. Taylor handed him the money, then turned to Christian. "What about you?"

"House Special for you, if you want." The bartender offered in an aside to Christian.

"No, thanks. I'll just stick to straight whiskey." Christian pulled several bills from his wallet and handed them over.

After he scooped up the money, the man nodded. "Sure thing."

Given the past few nights he'd had, Taylor didn't bother to go easy. He finished off his drink in record time, and as soon as the bartender had Christian's ready, Taylor asked for another. "You dance?"

"Yeah, I dance." Christian paused when the bartender leaned forward to get his attention.

"If you don't want the special, we do have live donors if you're interested. They're expensive, but clean."

"I think I'll stay sober tonight. Thanks for letting me know, though."

Taylor took his own drink from the bartender. "What does it feel like, to be bitten, I mean?" he asked Christian once they found a place along the wall.

"It's been a while since Mael fed from me, but it felt damn good. Led to some of the best sex I ever had."

Taylor nearly choked on his drink. "You've had sex with Mael?"

"He's the one who created me. He is also the one who owns me. I thought you knew that."

"Well, I did, but... I didn't know it went that far." He took another drink, muttering, "lucky bastard," under his breath.

"Not anymore. Cian doesn't like to share." Christian shrugged. "And it's not like there are any in Dio's court anywhere near Mael's caliber."

He couldn't resist it anymore. "Do you really have a fuck buddy when you go to Nigel's?"

"I used to, but not lately. Nigel never cared as long as my studies weren't affected."

Taylor knew it was the alcohol talking, otherwise he never would have continued the line of questioning. "Why not lately?"

"The last one tried to kill me." Christian gave Taylor a sidelong glance. "Don't tell Mael. He doesn't know about it."

Blinking, unsure if he even wanted to know, Taylor just stared at Christian. "What the hell happened?"

"The guy was more ambitious than I thought. He wanted to drain me, but I was lucky enough to figure it out before he could. Nigel took care of the rest. Since then, I haven't been bothered to follow through even when someone seems interested."

"That explains things." Taylor took another drink and closed his eyes. Without thinking about the ramifications, he draped one arm around Christian's shoulders. "Not everyone is like that."

"Gods, I hope not." Christian shifted the slightest bit to get more comfortable then settled again. "I don't want to be alone for the rest of my eternity. But for now, I get uneasy with most others, unless they're family. Nigel's told me to get over it, and I will. Eventually."

The alcohol buzzed through his brain, and Taylor forgot everything but the two of them. He leaned his head back against the wall and slipped his fingers through Christian's hair. "If I had any say in it, you wouldn't be."

"Well, in a way, you do. We'll be family. That is, if you visit me whenever Mael gets mad at me, and I have to high-tail it to Nigel." The touch appeared to relax Christian quite visibly, and he tilted his head toward Taylor's hand. "This is the first I've thought of it that way. Having you around will be great."

The line of Christian's throat begged for a kiss. Taylor wanted nothing more than to do just that. "I'm all yours," he muttered.

Those words brought a curious look to Christian's eyes. "You'll belong to Cian and Mael. I wouldn't forget it if I were you. So would you visit me at Nigel's?" He paused, lost in thought before he continued, "On second thought, you better not. I know he said he'd welcome you, but Nigel can be weird sometimes. Best to stay out of his way."

Taylor sighed, the whole mention of court politics bringing him swiftly back to his senses. "Yeah, you're right."

Chapter Thirteen

Cian had no idea what news could've prompted Mael to get out of bed so fast. All he knew from rumors around the palace was that they might have identified the person responsible for the were poisonings. Judging from the speculations he'd caught on the way to Mael's office, Cian figured no one knew who was behind it all. He opened the office door and closed it behind him.

"Okay. What on earth got you out of a post-orgasmic haze in two seconds flat?"

Head on his desk, Mael didn't look up or move in any way. "You could call it an internal memo from Sav."

Cian groaned and dropped into one of the chairs. "I'm not going to like this, am I?"

When he did look up, troubled wouldn't have been the word for his expression. It was worse. "The only good part is I can share the misery with you." A heavy sign escaped him as he closed his eyes and pinched the bridge of his nose. "Sav has irrefutable proof that Triarius' second companion, Apollonius, has been poisoning the were meat supply."

Cian shot out of his chair. "What!"

"I don't know why the hell he would, but there's no doubt it's him. I haven't spoken to anyone but you, and I'm trying to prepare myself to tell Dio."

Pacing, Cian struggled to keep himself in check. A rogue. A fucking rogue! And his hands were utterly tied, by Michael and Diocourides. "What proof is there? What about Triarius?"

"The were leader, Linda Ellsworth, identified him as the man who claimed to be from the Romanorum and helped them with their food supplies, specifically the ones that had been poisoned." Mael sat back in his seat, making a concerted effort for calm. "Sav also has a sworn statement from the wizard Apollonius bought the Silver Asperia from. There hasn't been much of an attempt on his part to hide his involvement with any of this."

"Do you think Triarius is behind it, too? If he's not, things are going to spiral very quickly out of control. Hell, even I've heard of the man's legendary temper. He's got me beat by a long shot in that department."

"There was no proof of that. I wouldn't even be coherent right now if it were that bad. I'm praying if he is, no proof ever shows up." Mael was being facetious, but Cian knew the headache would be phenomenal if Triarius was involved.

Cian stopped pacing and leaned on Mael's desk. "We have to tell Dio now. Everyone's already talking about who it could be. If even the slightest hint gets out, there's going to be hell to pay from every angle."

"The only ones who know are Sav, Linda, and I. Dio will find out in a few moments. I just wanted to prepare myself before I drop the bomb." Mael stood and stepped from behind his desk. "I would appreciate it if you joined me, love."

Cian caught him for a kiss. "Always." He sighed. "This isn't going to be pretty."

"As tempting as you are, duty comes first."

"I don't think I could get it up with this lovely bit of news in my head," Cian muttered.

"It's old age, my angel." As Mael headed out of the office, he turned back to wink at Cian. The attempt to lighten things wasn't working well, but Cian had to give the man credit for trying.

"Didn't hear you complain much earlier." Cian followed him, distinctly aware of a few others watching them both. He prayed no one had so much as an inkling of the truth behind the attacks. Another part of him hoped Triarius had absolutely nothing to do with any of it—if only for Brandon's sake.

"I can put up with a great deal." Mael encircled Cian's waist with one arm. No outward sign of distress showed on the prince's face as they walked the halls to Diocourides' study. Certain individuals had the right to disturb the eldest vampire at any time, and both Mael and Cian were two of them.

"I hope so," Cian murmured, "because the proverbial shit is about to hit the fan."

They both stopped at the door and Mael knocked. When he heard Dio say, "come in," he opened the door and they went inside. A pained expression crossed Mael's face when he saw Triarius and his companion, Lance, already there. Triarius nodded in greeting, while Lance smiled over at them. Cian barely bit back another groan. All they needed now was Memnet back from the grave.

Dio was in the midst of playing Scrabble with Josh and didn't notice them right away. "Ginormous is an approved word, I tell you. Check the dictionary."

"Good evening, gentlemen," Triarius said.

Mael inclined his head in polite greeting, then went straight to Dio. "Diocourides, I've received positive confirmation that Apollonius is responsible for the were poisonings in England."

Josh frowned as he sat back from the board. Dio eyed Mael with mild interest. "It seems I am going to have to investigate that boy on my own."

Cian cast a quick glance at Triarius and Lance. Lance's face had gone white. Triarius, on the other hand, had the look of a man in pure shock. Cian had the distinct feeling, were Triarius mortal, the man would've been sick. "We're sorry," Cian said, specifically to Triarius. Then a wave of undeniable heartbreak hit him, making him dizzy.

They hadn't known. They had no idea their lover had betrayed them.

It was clear from Dio's expression he felt the same shock of emotion. He went to Triarius. "This one I will deal with."

Mael stepped back, arm returning to Cian's waist. In a low voice, he asked, "Are you all right?"

Cian shook his head, still reeling. He watched Dio crouch in front of Triarius, who stared into space. "He didn't know," he whispered. "Neither of them did."

"I want to speak privately with my son and Lance," Dio said, dismissing the rest of them. Josh jumped up from his spot and headed out the door.

"I'll ensure word doesn't leak out, Diocourides." Mael drew Cian with him out of the room.

When the door closed, Cian fell against the wall, breathless and shaky. He'd never felt anything like that in all his lifetime. Shadows enveloped both of them and returned them to their private quarters. Mael snaked his arm around Cian and led him to the bed.

The moment they laid down, Cian curled around Mael and shuddered. "I felt it," he whispered. "Mael, I felt every thread of his heart break. I've never... never experienced anything so devastating."

"Diocourides is going to have to help him deal with it. I didn't think Triarius was behind it since he wouldn't have bothered coming to the Romanorum if his intentions weren't to change."

"In all my three thousand years, I've witnessed every facet of humanity, but nothing prepared me for that."

A wound opened at Mael's throat and he tipped Cian's head toward it. One with hand gripping Mael's fingers, Cian drank, needing to drown himself in his prince before everything else had a chance to burrow deeper inside. Soft murmurs of sound filled Cian's ears as he drank. The gentle tenor of Mael's thoughts blanketed Cian's mind with a sense of deeper tranquility. Every part of Cian flooded with Mael's essence, leaving room for little else.

* * *

"Son, we know little other than he's responsible for the poisonings." Dio realized after the shock wore off, Triarius would be in a rage, but for now it was enough to deal with the bewilderment he felt in his son.

Arms around Triarius' shoulders, Lance sighed as he pressed a soft kiss to Triarius' hair. "Love... please say something."

Triarius blinked up at Dio. "I gave him everything," he whispered. "We loved him."

"It isn't as easy for some to make this transition, Triarius." Dio had far more understanding of both vampire and human nature than any of his kind. Something had to be wrong, something more than the obvious. He cupped Triarius' cheek. "You know as well as I do, even when you give all, it isn't always as easy for those you give to."

"Your father is right," Lance said quietly. "We don't know why Apollonius did this, but something hasn't been right for a while. I think it's time to admit that, to ourselves and maybe to Diocourides."

"You can't jump to any conclusions." Dio glanced between Triarius and Lance, then continued, "Especially if you have been having problems. No reason to give me particulars if you don't want, but it would be best for me to handle this." His gaze returned to Triarius, hoping what he said would sink into his son.

"Apollonius has been distant for a while now," Lance said. "He avoids us, and then he seems to be gone on 'business' quite a bit." Triarius stood. Lance met Dio's gaze. "Triarius..."

An unfathomable, cold sort of calm filled the room. Triarius stared at nothing in particular. "I want him dead."

"What?" Lance jumped to his feet. "You can't be serious."

Triarius turned and a touch of his old, calculating self had returned. "I killed my son for threatening the Romanorum. I will *not* hesitate to do the same with a lover—especially a former one."

One brow rose, a sure sign Dio would brook no objection to his orders. "You most certainly did, son, after I had determined Aldrich couldn't be redeemed. *I* have yet to determine the same is true of Apollonius."

Triarius gritted his teeth, jaw going tight. Lance walked up to him and stood before him, cupping Triarius' face in both hands. He forced Triarius to look at him.

"You are one stubborn, sadistic son-of-a-bitch," Lance said, "and I refuse to let you do something as stupid as going against your father."

"Have I never explained why, Triarius?" It was rare for Dio to display true sadness, but for the briefest moment, he let it show. "My own Josh would have been destroyed but for the grace of the prince of San Diego. Josh was no more than a child when he was turned. You know such an act is against our laws. But Gabriel realized it was wiser for me to make the choice than those angered by Josh's existence. I know more of my children than anyone else. I know when it is time to destroy them, and when they can be saved. I allow the law to deal with some as it sees fit because my children need that structure, but when I can make the decision, I have to insist you let me." He glanced up at Triarius, silently pleading for understanding, "I can't let you destroy him until I know. If he can't be saved, you will deal with him."

Triarius closed his eyes. Then he opened them once more, calmer than before, and glanced from Lance to Dio. "I might argue, I might lose my temper..." He left Lance and knelt before Dio. "I would have been dead if you hadn't stepped in," he said, removing his mask. He met Dio's gaze. "But I will never disobey you."

The sadness fell from Dio and he reached out, hand gentle against his son's hair. "You are always free to argue and lose your temper, child. All I ask of you is understanding, just as I give it to you."

"You have it. That I can promise you."

"Thank you," Dio said with a smile. "I must attend to court. Take some time for yourselves."

* * *

Disgruntled, Christian glared at the half-empty bottle in his hand. The flat taste grated on his nerves more than usual. Maybe it was because he was deliberately breathing and catching Mael's scent. The prince stood not too far amongst the crowd surrounding Dio. Out of all of the smells, Christian could only focus on the one. He paid little attention to what was being said around him, and even less to any who wanted his attention. For the hundredth time, he told himself to ignore his own impulse. He didn't want to cause anymore trouble for his father.

"Hey," Taylor whispered, nudging him slightly. "You okay?"

He almost snarled at Taylor but managed to stop himself in time. "Yeah, I guess. Wanna ditch this session? I'm sure Mael and Cian won't mind."

Though he didn't look too convinced, Taylor nodded. "Sure. After you." Outside the throne room, things were surprisingly quiet for once. "So what's eating at you?"

"Nothing really important." A sigh escaped him as he held up the bottle. "I think I'm just getting a bit tired of the bottled thing. I shouldn't be as picky as I am, but I can't really help it."

Taylor grimaced. "Why drink that way then? I know you would rather have Mael, but there are others..."

"I've always been this way, Taylor. I'm not about to change now. I've only fed from family. I could find a mortal, but that's a responsibility I don't want yet." He tossed the bottle in a nearby trash can. Instead of heading outside, he decided to go to his room.

"Why not me then?"

Shocked, Christian halted and faced Taylor. "You? But you're Cian's. I don't think he'd like me snacking on you."

"In case you've forgotten, I'm still mortal, Christian." Taylor walked up to him, voice lowering. "But I'm also family. Why keep drinking out of a glass bottle when you have the chance to feed from a real person?"

"I haven't forgotten, but you don't seem to realize that Cian won't appreciate me feeding from you. I have no desire to run afoul of him again." Unable to suppress the image of Cian walking in on them and going off, Christian turned away from Taylor and continued on to his room.

Taylor grumbled and followed. He shut the bedroom door, giving them privacy. "Okay, first of all, how the hell would he know? Second, why can't you trust me? Why push me away when I try to help?"

"I do trust you, Taylor. How in hell did you get the idea that I don't?" Christian plopped into the nearest chair and scowled. "I am not pushing you away, but you're insane if you think you can hide something like that from either Mael or Cian."

Taylor sprawled out on Christian's bed. "Fine. Keep drinking out of those damned bottles."

"Now you're mad at me."

"I'm not mad," Taylor said. "Just... frustrated. I care about you, Christian. I know you hate drinking like that, and I want to help."

With a heavy sign, Christian got up and joined Taylor on the bed, sitting beside him. "I'm sorry. I'm just afraid of Cian getting mad again like he did the last time." He gave Taylor a half-ass smile. "Kind of makes me walk on egg shells, you know."

"Have you thought about the fact that, feeding from me, in Cian's eyes, would mean you aren't feeding from Mael?"

He turned his head away from Taylor to hide the sadness. "I don't feed from Mael anymore. If I did, I wouldn't be whining now. Never mind. It's not that fucking important."

"Hey." Taylor tugged Christian down to lay beside him, arms going around Christian's shoulders. "I'm sorry. Okay? I just don't like seeing you miserable."

A bit of a smile played about his lips as he shook off the disquiet. He stretch out and rested his head on Taylor's chest to listen to the strong beat of the mortal's heart. "Believe me, I'm happier than I was before you showed up. You're somebody I can be myself with. It means more than I think you understand."

Taylor threaded his fingers through Christian's hair. It felt good. "You're the first true friend I've had," he said quietly. "I would do anything for you."

"You know, I've been feeling lost, but it's not so bad as long as you're around. It doesn't go away even when we argue. You're the only one I can talk to as freely as I do."

"I'm always here when you need me." Taylor lifted Christian's head until their eyes met. "I promise you that."

* * *

Apologizing had never been an issue. Cian had no trouble doing so any other time, and he wasn't the type to avoid admitting when he was wrong. This time, however, it seemed harder. A part of him—quite a large part—realized just how much damage he'd caused. He only prayed Christian would hear him out. He knocked on Christian's door, smiling slightly when he heard Taylor's voice. They'd become friends, and for that, Cian was grateful. He hadn't realized just how grateful until Mael had explained Christian's current situation.

The door opened and Taylor blinked in surprise. "Cian?"

"Could I possibly speak to Christian? Privately?"

Taylor stepped aside and cast a glance at Christian. "I'll be in my room if you need me, Christian."

For a split second, Christian looked like he didn't want Taylor to leave, but he turned away to pour himself a glass of blood. The glance he gave Cian was calm but guarded. "Hey, Cian."

Cian stopped Taylor before the young man could leave. "Stay. He needs you," Cian murmured. Taylor nodded and closed the door before sitting on the bed. Cian knew he wasn't particularly welcome, so he chose to remain where he stood, if only to reassure Christian. "To say I owe you an apology is..." He shook his head. "Inadequate."

Christian held up a hand before Cian could continue. "It's not necessary, Cian. Really it isn't. I got over it, and I'm fine with the way things are. To say I really don't give a damn wouldn't be putting a fine point on it."

Cian sighed. "You're as stubborn as your father." He gave Christian his own smile to soften the words. "But it is necessary. I love Mael with every ounce of my soul. However, I also know you love him as well. He loves you." His gaze fell on Taylor, who sat silently watching them both. "I didn't understand the connection until... someone put it into perspective for me. There is nothing I wouldn't do for Taylor. The same holds true for Mael where you are concerned. I'm not human, but I'm learning."

"I wouldn't worry about it, Cian." Christian took a long swallow from the glass before he added, "I really am fine with the way things are. It's not that big of a deal. It was at first, but I'm a grown man. It's time I manage on my own anyway. My grandfather agrees."

"As you wish. Just know that I am sorry." Cian motioned for Taylor and when the young man was close enough, Cian whispered, "don't make the mistake I did." At Taylor's questioning look, Cian smiled. "Don't wait too long to follow your heart."

Having ignored their private conversation, Christian drained his glass and set it down. "I appreciate your apology. And I owe you one as well for being as angry as I was at first."

"Apology accepted," Cian said. Then he bowed and left the room, feeling a bit better. He'd gotten the impression that Christian wanted more than anything to maintain distance, and he couldn't fault him for it. For now, though, he had an appointment with his prince and Diocourides. Now that they were in Rome, it was time to focus on Taylor's turning, preferably before anything else came down on their heads.

The door to Mael's office stood open and Cian smiled when he saw his prince behind the desk. He walked in and shut the door behind him. "I'm sorry I'm late," he said as he sat down in the chair beside Diocourides.

"We were just talking about the progress Cornelius and I have made in your request, Cian. Help yourself to some wine, if you want."

"I'm gathering it wasn't as difficult as they thought it would be." Mael poured a glass for Cian and held it out to him.

Cian laughed and took a sip. "How well did our court mage manage to contain himself at the prospect anyway?"

"As well as I have." Dio gave him a gleeful smile. "We've been successful so far, but it's not complete. Not yet time to get your hopes up."

"Though it seems Cornelius and you can't help getting yours up." Mael chuckled. "I knew both of you would be delighted with his project."

"Angel blood and vampire blood is a very intriguing combination. It's been a task and a half to figure out how to make them compatible." It didn't look like Dio minded at all.

"I imagine so." Cian took another drink. "Does it help in the least that I carry Mael's blood within me as well?"

"It's made it easier, but doesn't solve all the problems. Still, I have no doubt we'll have what you both want within the next few weeks. It would be sooner, but Cornelius complains he can't get time in his workroom like he wants. Only he isn't quite so polite about phrasing it." Dio broke out into laughter. "He's very colorful."

"Now there's an understatement if I ever heard one," Cian chuckled. "At least Brandon keeps him sane. Relatively speaking."

"I don't think we're in too much of a hurry, though I'm sure you both don't want to waste a great deal of time. I hope you two have discussed all of this with Taylor." Dio glanced between them with an inquiring look.

"We've been waiting to hear from you regarding progress," Cian said. "Taylor knows it will include blood from both of us, but beyond that, unless Christian's explained things in more detail, we've not had the chance."

Mael shrugged. "Christian wouldn't discuss it without permission from us. I was going to let Cian deal with the explanations since the two of them are closer."

"Thanks," Cian laughed. "You've been doing this father bit longer than I have." He thought for a moment. "Wait. Scratch that. I've never done this before."

"There is already a connection between the two of you, love." Mael rested his hand on Cian's. "We can both discuss it with him if you want, warn him of the potential danger. I want him completely willing with no doubts. Or as few doubts as possible."

"I agree with you, Mael. I won't allow this to be done unless the boy fully understands the risks as well as the benefits."

"Absolutely," Cian said. "Personally, it will be a first for me as well. I've never witnessed a turning."

"It's not the easiest thing to go through, but we'll be together."

Dio nodded and said, "I'll ensure your quarters are guarded when the time comes. There will be a great deal of curiosity over Taylor's creation, but I will keep most of it to a minimum."

"Thank you." Cian turned his hand over and threaded his fingers with Mael's. "I know he's nervous. I certainly am."

Chapter Fourteen

Seated at his desk, sipping brandy while he read over the latest news from London, Diocourides thanked the gods for even this briefest moment of peace. The Romanorum had been in a state of semi-chaos since Mael and Cian had arrived. People still held doubts about Mael's companion, but Dio had spent more than enough time with them both to know Cian was as trustworthy—if not more so—than the members of the Romanorum itself. Just as Dio took another sip of his drink, someone knocked on his office door.

"Come in."

The door opened and no less than five court members entered. From their expressions alone, Dio had the distinct feeling he'd be fielding yet more complaints about Mael's partner. One of the members shut the door, and stepped up to speak.

"Diocourides," the woman said, "we have reason to believe that Cian Carmichael is responsible for the poisonings and stakings in London and here in Rome."

Dio almost choked on his brandy, and only by sheer willpower did he manage to not spit it across his desk. "What?"

"The sorcerer has the power and the means to poison entire tribes," one of the men said. "Not to mention, he is a known vampire hunter."

"And do you have any proof of this?"

"There are rumors-"

"Rumors are not fact," Dio interrupted as gently as possible. "We have leads on the case, and none of them point in any fashion to Carmichael."

"But what about the stakings?" the first woman asked. "He killed many vampires in London before he entered Prince Black's court." The others nodded in unison.

Dio sighed. "Cian did the Romanorum a great service by disposing of rogues who would have destroyed our way of life." Before any of them could say a word, he continued. "Might I also add that he played a very instrumental role in Memnet's defeat—including sacrificing his own life to save Mael Black."

"How did he return then?"

Unsure how to answer the question without revealing Cian's true nature, Dio took the most objective approach possible. "Because he is a sorcerer. He possesses magic and abilities many do not, and his love and devotion are what fueled his return to Mael Black's side.

"What about the rumors that he cast a spell on Prince Black?"

"He did nothing of the sort." Dio stood and went to open his office door. "I appreciate your concern—all of you, but rumors have no place in these halls. Cian Carmichael is an ally to the Romanorum, and a very devoted companion to Mael Black. Now, if you all will excuse me," he said, gesturing subtly for them to leave, "I have matters to attend to."

"Yes, Diocourides." The woman bowed, and the others followed suit.

Dio waited until they were down the hall before shutting his office door. He rested his forehead against it and groaned. He had things that needed discussing, but more with Cian than Mael at the moment. He wondered as he sent out a silent call to have Cian join him if the angel knew about the stories running throughout the palace. He poured two glasses of brandy and sat down in one of the more comfortable chairs to wait. When the door opened once more, he smiled up at Cian.

"Please, have a seat and join me." He handed Cian the other glass of brandy.

"Thank you." Cian took a sip and sat down, regarding him curiously. "Okay, I give. What's going on?"

Dio chuckled. "You've become a popular fellow since your arrival."

One blond eyebrow rose. "You could say that." Realization seemed to dawn on Cian and he groaned. "Let me guess: I'm either guilty of poisoning or bewitching Mael."

"Both, actually," Dio said with a grin. "Oh, and apparently you've been busy staking vamps as well."

Cian's bright blue eyes widened. "Where do they come up with this stuff?"

"I could speculate, namely around the notion of jealousy, but it won't stop the rumors." Dio sipped his drink, momentarily lost in thought. "Does Mael know any of this?"

"Yes. There's nothing we hide from one another."

Dio nodded. "While I would hope that no one is foolish enough to so much as think about laying a finger on you, I suggest caution."

"I couldn't agree more."

* * *

Christian understood what his father planned to do. The mixture of Mael and Cian's blood to be used in turning Taylor would cause an uproar if it were known. Troubled, he drummed his fingertips against his thigh as he waited for his grandfather to enter and begin the court session. The notion didn't bother him. He wasn't a snob about those kinds of things, but Christian also realized very few would agree with him. Some of the younger vampires didn't consider bloodlines a big deal; however, to the older ones, it was everything. And the halls of Romanorum were filled with quite a few old vampires.

A third formula, whom Christian knew somewhat, came closer and signaled for Christian's attention. He eyed the redhead and waited to hear whatever it was Malatesta wanted.

"Black, I wanted to ask if you would speak to your grandfather on my father's behalf. He wishes to return to Rome. We would be most grateful."

No more than mild inquiry showed on Malatesta's features, but grateful meant anything Christian could essentially say whatever he wanted, which meant Malatesta was desperate for help. Christian sympathized with the vampire since one did not fail one's creator.

"I'll ask Prince Nigel what he thinks about the matter, and I'll let you know as soon as I can."

The comment earned Christian a deep bow from Malatesta before she straightened and turned on her heel. Christian stared at the glass resting on his other thigh. The smallest motion of his hand made the red liquid swirl, staining the crystal clear glass in a light wash of blood. Another vampire approached, a leering gaze sweeping over Christian. Christian ignored him and the blonde went away. He had zero interest in fucking anybody.

No one knew the full truth about Cian, which would only make it worse. To those who thought like his grandfather, one did not mix blood with any other creature but mortal and vampire. Christian closed his eyes and said a little prayer that Taylor's true parentage never got out. It would be a nightmare, and Taylor didn't deserve it.

Thoughts of Taylor disturbed Christian. He liked the guy, a lot. Just the notion made him wince as he took a sip of blood. If he were truthful with himself, he'd never felt so close to another, except for Mael.

"What did Malatesta want?"

The voice intruded on Christian's thoughts, and he glanced up to see one of the most notorious court gossips hovering near him. The primped and painted face of the man and his lace and velvet clothing spoke of having lived two centuries ago. It wasn't unusual for many of the older ones to wear the fashions of their mortal life.

Christian offered him a fake smile. "We discussed overthrowing Nigel. Why? Do you want in on it?"

Du Bourg tittered. "Such a bon mot, Black."

Christian gave him a fake smile and kept a bland gaze fixed on the vampire. A moment later the creature got the clue. After he bowed to Christian, he walked away to join one of the circle of vampires near the dais. Left alone to his thoughts, he reflected on his attraction to others in the past. None had been friends with him. They were lovers, pure and simple physical release. When it was time to move on, Christian moved on without a backward glance. Only Mael had commanded Christian's emotions.

Taylor made things different. The whole situation confused Christian every which way. As much as he might want to return Taylor's interest, it was best he didn't. Mael had an incredible jealous streak, and Christian had been the recipient of it many times. He doubted if that had changed. Add Cian's possible reaction to the mix, and it was all doomed before it could start.

The moment Nigel entered and made his way to his throne, Christian shoved his worries aside. There was no excuse for not being alert during the court proceedings. He stood with the others, smiled, and bowed his head in respect to his grandfather.

Nigel motioned for Sinclair, his eldest advisor, to approach the dais. He acknowledged Christian's brief smile with a nod of his head, then gestured for his grandson to sit beside him. Once Christian had taken his proper place in the smaller chair near his own, he nodded to Sinclair to begin.

"The church has told us they are not involved in the twelve stakings we've had over the last month. I, and others, am not convinced of the church's innocence, your Excellency. Many of us remember the Holy Sons."

A ripple of whispers followed Sinclair's pronouncement. Some agreed with him while most gave little credence to the latest rumor mill. However, the alarm over the stakings had risen and was indeed in many faces.

"Are you certain it isn't that sorcerer, Carmichael?" a voice called out from the midst of the others.

"He needs to be held accountable by Diocourides," Another insisted.

Nigel held up a hand for silence. "Security has been called in from other regions, and the number of our enforcers has doubled. My son, Prince Mael, has provided irrefutable proof the Holy Sons were disbanded just as his Holiness has claimed. There is no reason to anger our allies in the church by allowing others to spread this nonsense." He refrained from mentioning Carmichael, but many in his court knew how he felt about his son's current companion. "We will discuss this later in my study, Sinclair."

"As you wish, your Excellency."

The whispering around them died down as Sinclair brought up the next topic they needed to discuss. "There are two complaints of mistreatment against Claudio Monti, brought by the mortals Norma Miller and Aidan Taylor."

"Has this been investigated?" Nigel asked before he glanced over at his grandson. While Christian's attempt to hide his distraction from the others was successful, Nigel knew the boy too well. Something troubled Christian, and it made Nigel curious. What had Mael done this time?

The barriers Christian erected kept others from prying, and his skills were impressive. Nigel hadn't tried to read him for a long time, and the boy had improved beyond measure. None of those around them would be able to penetrate Christian's protection. To any watching Nigel, it would seem Sinclair had his full attention. He had little tolerance for his kind mistreating their donors and dealt with it with little thought. He focused his mind on his grandson to read the young vampire.

On the surface, Nigel sensed Christian's struggle between acceptance for the creature Mael had chosen, and jealousy of Cian. Part of the boy longed for his father back, not at all unusual since Christian still loved Mael a great deal. While the child hid some anger over Nigel's interference in drugging and putting him in Mael's bed, he was secretly disappointed the ploy hadn't worked.

Nigel could also sense Christian's trepidation over how things were developing with Taylor and worry over his own emotions for Taylor. It wasn't hard to delve through the tangle of confusion about Mael and the burgeoning feelings Christian had toward Mael's newest, but there was something else. It didn't matter how hard the boy tried to hide anything, it wouldn't work.

Something about Taylor bothered Christian. No, not exactly bothered. It made him fearful for his soon-to-be brother. It wasn't long before Nigel unraveled the full thread of thought. Diocourides and Mael's magician were working to combine Mael and Cian's blood to use with the formula to turn Taylor.

Angel blood? Cian Carmichael was an angel as well? The only outward sign of his temper was the slight stiffening of his body, but his outrage verged on madness. There were no words for such a crime. How dare his son consider an offense to their blood! That boy would be no more than an abomination, and rightly so.

It was the association with that damn sorcerer. His own son had so far forgotten himself, he no longer cared what was due to his line. In that moment, Nigel severed his relationship with Mael. No son of his would associate with anything like Carmichael and contemplate creating a monstrosity.

If applying to Diocourides didn't bring them to their senses, Nigel had other methods at his disposal.

Chapter Fifteen

"How long, do you think, before they'll have no time for you?"

The words echoed through Apollonius' mind, unending. It seemed like ages ago since he'd left Triarius and Lance, and the longer he stayed away, the stronger the anger became. He'd heard the whispers, thanks to various sources, about his mental state. He scowled at the ceiling. Let them all believe what they wished. Plans had been set in motion that no one could possibly foresee.

No one, except his single ally in this whole fucked-up mess. Nigel might be something of an aid, but Apollonius had much stronger dealings with another that surpassed anything Nigel could ever hope to match. Over the last several months, he'd forged his own alliance with someone far more powerful than even Diocourides.

"Are they still that important to you?"

A restless stirring inside Apollonius accompanied the words. Seth, one of the ancient Egyptian gods, now used Apollonius' body as a host. Apollonius was more than glad to have the being within him. He'd come to rely on the sense of another to the point where he wasn't sure how he'd ever tolerated being without Seth.

"In truth, no," Apollonius admitted out loud. "The importance they once held is gone. Soon enough, they—along with the rest of the damned Romanorum—will be nothing but a vague memory." He realized he'd be lying if he said the sex had sucked. Quite the contrary. Now, though, he barely remembered what a kiss felt like. Grumbling, he shoved those thoughts away.

"We have plans to accomplish, and you think of sex?" A soft ripple of laughter filled Apollonius' mind. *"I suppose I could take care of it, but we do have more important things to do."*

"You try having a sexy-as-sin god inside you and see how focused you can be," Apollonius muttered.

"Poor Apollonius. Shall I relieve you or let you suffer?" Seth's black energy covered Apollonius and warmth flooded his skin with the small rush of power. *"I did so want to discuss the odds of your little friend, Nigel, bringing us the sorcerer. I always have back-up plans just in case."*

Apollonius gasped, every inch of his flesh tingling. "Nigel is not my friend," he growled. "But if he doesn't get Carmichael, then we use other means at our disposal." He shuddered. "Fucking tease."

"He's motivated enough with all the rumors we've been spreading. Image is all to his sort." Tingling pulses ghosted through Apollonius from his mind to his toes. The resonance filled him with an encompassing sense of Seth, soothing something within him, yet arousing him at the same time. *"But still, I have another idea should this one fall through. Our ace in the hole, as it were. I believe Diocourides' sweetheart will be of use to us. What is his name again?"*

"Josh..." Apollonius struggled to keep track of the conversation, but whatever Seth was doing, it was quickly winning out. He ran his hand over his torso, stopping just above the waistband of his jeans, which had become rather snug in the past few minutes. "Tell me more..." He no longer cared if Seth wanted to talk business, so long as the man... being... kept doing what he was doing.

"See to it, Apollonius. I want him at the same time we get Carmichael." Heat followed in the wake of Apollonius' hand, burning through the material as a soft chuckle echoed in his thoughts. *"Does it feel good?"* Seth asked before he continued. *"A few more whispers in the right ears won't hurt either. It's time everybody thinks either the sorcerer or Diorcourides are behind our stakings. Too many have the mistaken notion it's the Holy Sons. What people will believe is astounding, isn't it?"*

Moaning softly, Apollonius let his hand roam lower until his palm covered the bulge in his jeans. "Keep doing that," he murmured, "and I'll obey your every command..."

"Of course, you will. You're mine." With the last two words, a sharp sensation surged through Apollonius. The stamp of Seth's presence had taken him over, and in its wake, tantalizing shimmers of a pleasure Apollonius had never know. *"Unzip your pants."*

Apollonius didn't hesitate. In fact, he exceeded. His jeans hit the floor and he spread his legs, eyes shut as he reveled in the sensations coursing through him. His cock flexed the moment he touched it. "Yours."

"We've an eternity together, you and I." The sheer force of Seth's power warmed every part of Apollonius with incredible heat. It felt as if another hand guided his with each stroke of his fingers. *"Nothing and no one will interfere with us."*

Apollonius simply gave up talking. He sucked three fingers into his mouth, then reached down, thrusting them into his ass. Hips jerking upward, he pumped himself faster, all thoughts focused on the being residing within him. "Seth..."

Deep satisfaction flooded Apollonius, and he knew it came from Seth. The Egyptian god was pleased with him. Apollonius could have sworn there was more emotion to Seth now than he'd ever noticed before. A soft groan sounded in his thoughts as if Seth were as affected as Apollonius. Ghost hands joined his, urging him on harder until nothing remained in his mind but his own need and the dark appetite of the god.

Shadows slithered around Apollonius, though he felt Seth controlling them more than himself. He pulled his legs up and his eyes rolled as thickness filled him alongside his own fingers. The strokes on his cock quickened, and for the briefest second, a face flashed behind his closed eyes. A dark, seductive gaze held him and he shouted, entire body jerking as he came harder than he thought possible.

The intensity lingered seconds longer than it should have, holding Apollonius and Seth enthralled. Both were as aware of each other as they were of themselves. The black energy writhed around Apollonius.

While Apollonius lay, panting, he felt the sensation of Seth stretching within him. Just to see him again, he closed his eyes. The dark seduction had been replaced with something Apollonius hadn't expected. Was it possible? Eyes still shut, Apollonius felt himself fall into the enigmatic gaze. He'd sworn off everything before meeting Seth, but this changed it all. They had to succeed. He wouldn't let his... lover down.

* * *

"Why isn't Diocourides doing anything about these stakings?" Acilia De Luca's angry expression marred the perfection of her ice blonde beauty. She was the daughter of one of Dio's most prominent advisors. "My father believes the sorcerer Carmichael is behind them."

Christian knew the angel would do no such thing. Cian had killed rogues, which was a far cry from staking law-abiding vampires. If he knew anything about Cian, he knew the man did make distinctions between the two. He might waffle on his emotions toward the guy, but he knew Cian was a decent person. "He only killed rogues, De Luca. Most of you don't know how much he's done for us."

"Of course, you'd defend him, Black. He's your father's companion." She sneered at him.

"I wouldn't defend him if I knew he was guilty." Christian shrugged.

"It could be Diocourides." Malco Giordano joined the conversation with his own snide comment. The vampire, dressed in an impeccable gray designer suit, displayed both his lineage and prestige in the proud carriage of his body.

"Are you crazy, Giordano?" His companion, Ella Moretti, chastised him as she shook her head. From red head to designer-clad foot, she was as well dressed as Giordano. "You can't say that in public."

"Sure I can. I just did. Black's father has already proven it wasn't the church, and I don't think the sorcerer did it either. Why would he fuck a vampire prince and kill legal vampires behind everybody's back? Makes no sense."

Acilia gave him a doubtful look. "Why would the father of us all do something like that?"

"To get rid of a few problems. Wilson Everett was staked two days ago. All of us know how vehement he's been against many of the improvements Diocourides wants. Simple process of elimination." Giordano made it all sound very logical. "He's not the only one who's disagreed with Diocourides who's been staked."

Christian made the most logical argument he could against the idea. "At any given time, twenty percent of the Romanorum disagree with him, if not more. The majority of them are still here. Diocourides would never kill someone over a disagreement."

"True." Ella snickered. "Advisor De Luca is a thorn in Diocourides' side, and he still lives."

"Very true." De Luca laughed. Everybody knew her father even opposed Diocourides once in a while for the fun of it.

"I'm not the only one who thinks Diocourides is behind it." Giordano gave the others a knowing look, then lowered his voice. "Prince Amanda and first formula Alvarez say he is. I heard them say that's the way it should be, and I agree with him. Diocourides is our ruler. He does what he wants."

"So I suppose it doesn't matter. If it's him, it's his right," Acilia pronounced. The others nodded at her words.

"I doubt if it's him." That's all Christian would say. He couldn't argue with the rest since it was Diocourides' right, whether he took advantage of it or not. He walked away from the others and headed toward the throne room. It was near session time, and he hoped to catch Diocourides before the vampire began the session. Luck was with him, and he found Dio approaching the throne room doors alone. "Diocourides.

"Hello, Christian. How can I help you?"

"I just wanted to let you know about the things I've been overhearing. There are rumors Cian is behind the stakings.

People are saying it's either him or you eliminating your enemies."

Dio rolled his eyes in response. "What is it with my children? The church is cleared, now I have to clear Cian and myself?"

Christian didn't expect Dio to ask for any names, and he didn't. He just motioned for Christian to enter as the doors opened for them. Christian slipped inside and played least in sight against the back wall. The others parted down the center of the crowd for Dio to walk to his throne. When he reached it, he turned and sat on the topmost step. Before anyone could say anything, Darius De Luca stepped forward.

"Yes, De Luca? What is it now?"

The silver-haired vampire appeared calm and collected, but his voice carried notes of anger. "When are you going to do something about the deaths, Diocourides? Are you going to let the sorcerer continue to roam free while our own die at his hand?"

"First it was the church, now it's Cian Carmichael? I understand some of you believe it's me." Dio eyed those assembled around him with a wry look. "Who else will you blame with no proof at this rate?"

"I know it's Cian Carmichael. He's killed vampires before. We all know it, yet he's allowed in our midst. It's insane," De Luca argued. Some of the others nodded to show their agreement.

Dio watched them whisper among themselves while he grew very quiet. A moment later, many in the room shifted uneasily. Although he kept his tone quiet and reasonable, he dared any of them to refute what he said with a look. "I know

Cian Carmichael very well. He is no danger to those who obey our laws." The whispers ceased. "I would never allow any among my children who would harm you. Carmichael is not behind the stakings, nor am I. I have no desire to punish any, but I will do so if anything of this nature reaches my ears." Not a vampire moved as Dio pinned each one with a severe gaze. "My word is the last to be spoken on the subject. I know you all understand me."

* * *

"Tell Diocourides I must speak with him." Nigel scowled at the servant when the young man didn't move fast enough. "Now!"

The servant pushed open the throne room doors. "Diocourides, Prince Nigel is here to see you."

Once the rest of the court members had exited, Diocourides motioned for Nigel. "Thank you."

Nigel strode up to the dais and barely waited for the door to close. His closest court members stood behind him. "My son has crossed the line," he snapped.

Diocourides regarded him with a serious, if curious, expression. "How so?"

"Taylor Reed must not be allowed to turn."

"Your opinion, while valued, is not going to change anything, Nigel."

"Crossbreeding is abhorrent. Taylor Reed will become nothing but an abomination."

"Your obsession with purity in bloodlines is clouding your judgment."

"There is no purity when a vampire breeds with an-" Nigel stopped himself before he said another word. While he knew damn well what the sorcerer was, his court members did not. He stepped forward, voice lowering. "If you allow this to happen, I will not hesitate to make Cian Carmichael's true identity known."

Dio's expression hardened. "I do not respond well to blackmail."

"And I refuse to permit my son to taint our bloodline with such a disgusting abomination."

Dio rose, eyes going dark. "You will not threaten me, Nigel. Do I make myself clear? Nor will you interfere with Taylor's turning."

"As Mael's father, it is my right!"

A thunderous look flashed across Dio's face. "If you do not put an end to these protests and threats, I will have your position stripped out from under you. You will lose your throne, and all of Rome."

Nigel blinked. "How can you consider such a thing? I am the head of this family!"

"And I am the father of all of you!"

Nigel sensed those behind him growing nervous. He gritted his teeth. If he couldn't get Dio to stop the turning, then he would find another way to deal with Mael's insolence. "Understood."

"Leave me. You have much to think about."

* * *

"I've already spoken to Taylor about everything that will happen during his turning and after."

Christian nodded. He hadn't told his father about any of the rumors he'd heard. Mael was worried enough about Taylor's turning. "I'll be there to help if it's okay with you."

"Cian and I very much want you there. We're a family, Christian. You as well as Taylor and Cian." Mael smiled as he caught Christian's arm and pulled him close for a hug. "As the eldest, you'll have to set a good example. I think you both have become close friends."

"It's hard not to like the guy, dad." He rested his head against Mael's chest. Mael had always represented safety and security. It didn't matter if they'd had their problems. Mael was always there when Christian needed him

"I'm also relying on you to protect him when I'm elsewhere, child.

"I will." While Christian wasn't as powerful as many in the Romanorum, he could drag Taylor with him to a deep section of the shadows only his own family could enter. "Don't worry so much, Mael. I'm not like Amael. I would never harm Taylor. I will protect him with my life if I have to."

"My apologies. I know that. I'm just worried about many things, Christian."

"Were you as worried when I was turned?" Christian asked, curious. All he could recall was a calm, unflappable Mael at the time.

Mael made a face. "Yes, I was. I didn't show it to you."

Christian laughed and patted Mael's shoulder. "Everything will go exactly as it's supposed to. Taylor will be fine, and he'll grow up and leave the nest before you can blink."

"Thanks for the helpful piece of advice, smart ass." Mael ruffled Christian's hair.

Christian stole another hug before he pulled away. "Time to see Nigel. He wants me there during his session tonight."

"Join us when you can tomorrow night, son."

"I will."

Christian summoned the shadows, arriving in his grandfather's home. When he entered Nigel's antechamber, however, he froze. Never in his existence had he seen such a look of malevolence on his grandfather. A chill raced through him. Did Nigel know the truth about Cian and Taylor?

As if in answer, Nigel said in a perfectly controlled, cold voice, "I know what that thing is. I won't have its blood tainting mine."

"But, grandfather..."

"Silence!" Nigel roared. "Diocourides refuses to do anything about this atrocity. So be it. If I must, I will reclaim what is mine. How can my son stoop so low as to consort with a hunter who isn't even human. An angel! How dare he!"

Horrified, Christian opened his mouth to say something, but nothing came out. His grandfather couldn't mean what he thought Nigel meant. The dismay deepened with the realization Nigel knew the truth about Cian.

Infuriated, Nigel stood and paced in front of his chair. Hatred and malice dripped from every word he uttered. "A vampire and an angel. Allowed to create a child. I have no choice. To allow something like that to exist is..." He scowled at Christian.

"Taylor is just as worthy as any of your children, grandfather."

"Do not speak to me. I have yet to decide if you will be punished for knowing what Carmichael was and not telling me. I will not hesitate to reclaim your blood as well should you disappoint me again."

A strong sense of Nigel's power engulfed Christian. Its very savagery frightened him. At that very moment, the relatively short distance from his father became an insurmountable gulf. Nigel could, in a split second, attack and drain Christian. There would be little Christian could do to prevent him. Nor could Mael save him.

"Our line will remain as untainted as it has been for millennium. I will take care of your father, then I will deal with Carmichael." The words were all the more chilling for their lack of emotion. "I'm not the only one who hates the sorcerer. It wasn't hard to find others willing to get rid of him for me. As for Mael, I will take back what is mine."

All Christian could do was remain as still as a statue while Nigel continued his rant against Mael and Cian. He was a silent witness to Nigel's plan to destroy them, and he was too afraid to move lest his grandfather turn the rage on him.

Chapter Sixteen

Mael knew the potential problems with creating another child. It was the reason he only had one child at a time. He'd learned his lesson when he'd had to destroy Amael. The chance of jealousy and severe problems could arise. He knew Christian felt left out and very much an outsider because Mael no longer allowed for a physical relationship between them. Nothing Mael said so far had changed Christian's perceptions. Everything was still the same, at least to Mael, but he had yet to convince his son of the fact. At least Christian liked Taylor and had promised to protect him

Mael had sent Cian to bed for a few hours of sleep. It would be a long vigil, watching over Taylor until he woke up. Mael needed the time to bond with their son. Up until now, he really hadn't had a chance to, though he was aware Cian grown close to the mortal. His senses kept track of the minute signs indicating Taylor rapidly approached death.

With his power, Mael kept Taylor's mind insulated from the reality of what was happening. The last time he had done this was over ninety years ago. He'd not forgotten the process, but the intensity of his own emotional reactions had faded. Now they returned, crystal clear. He traced his own power and blood through Taylor. *His child.* The two words had a power all their own. Mael also detected Cian's essence. The odd signature of his angel within Taylor increased the tenor of Mael's feelings.

There was a chance Taylor wouldn't survive the change. Mael had warned both Cian and Taylor. As he closed his eyes, Mael acknowledged the tie binding them. If Taylor didn't return from his death, it would make everything much harder. Mael had known all of it when he'd agreed to Cian wanting a child.

"You will return, my child, and I will be waiting for you."

With the cessation of Taylor's breath, Mael's eyes opened. He reached for Taylor's lifeless hand and held it tightly. Oh, how hard he prayed. He needed the time alone to deal with the fear, and keep it hidden from Cian. It would be at least two nights before they would know if the formula had been successful.

He lifted Taylor's hand to his lips and brushed a soft kiss to the rapidly cooling flesh. Stiffness would soon set in, but decay would not. Even if Taylor didn't wake up, his body wouldn't decompose now. Returning the hand to the bed cover, he gently caressed Taylor's forehead, pushing back the long, unruly brown hair. The bond with Taylor took on its own rich edge, that of Father and child. It was the knowledge that his blood gave life to another.

Mael felt Diocourides' presence when the eldest entered the room, but he didn't turn to look. Dio's hand rested on his shoulder. "It begins."

When he felt the light squeeze on his shoulder, he glanced back at Dio. "Others will be able to sense the difference in him."

"I know. Word will be sent out to everyone else. There will be no problems concerning Taylor. If any do arise, they will deal with me, Mael." To some of their own kind, Taylor would be an abomination, something they wouldn't be unable to understand. Mael knew Dio wanted any potential trouble of that kind dealt with before anything got out of hand.

"Thank you for everything you've done, Diocourides. Cian and I are grateful..."

Dio cut him off before Mael could finish. "Nonsense, my boy. I was only too eager to jump in and see if it could be done." He chuckled. "It's been an experience working with Cornelius. Absolutely brilliant man, though a bit testy when things don't go his way."

Mael laughed. "My magician is one of a kind. I hope Aristotle left your belongings alone."

"At last count, I'm missing one of my rings and a book on transmutation compounds, and I believe Joshua is missing one of his belts."

"I will make sure they are returned."

"Don't bother, my boy. If Aristotle can find a use for them, he can have them. And Mael, don't worry so much." Dio gave him a shrewd look. "I have a feeling this young man will surprise all of us."

Once again alone, Mael's gaze returned to the lifeless form on the bed. For the next two nights, he would never be far from Taylor. If he woke up... Mael hastily changed his thoughts. *When* Taylor woke up, only his fathers and Christian would be allowed to attend him. It would be a few weeks before Mael would let anybody else near Taylor. Taylor had to be isolated for his own safety, both from other vampires and for the safety of mortals.

* * *

Mael had kept an intent eye on Taylor even during the times he rested. His whispered words filled an unreceptive mind, but still he maintained the contact. Knowing the time would be soon, he forced his body to awaken. He dressed quickly and went the short distance down the hall to Taylor's room. He didn't need the sight of his angel sitting beside the bed to tell him Cian was anxious. He felt the tendrils of the sorcerer's thoughts in his own.

"Soon," Cian murmured, brushing Taylor's forehead with his fingers. "Please tell me it'll be soon, Mael. I want him back."

"It will be, Cian. It takes time for the body to adjust and the formula to work." He stood behind Cian and laid his hand on his angel's shoulder. This was always the worst time. The waiting. And the chance Taylor would never awaken. There was no way to tell if he would or not. Not until Taylor's mind tried to reach out for Mael.

Tilting his head, Cian nuzzled Mael's hand with his cheek, eyes never leaving Taylor's face. He remained that way for several minutes before a slight mental tug cut through the worry. Gasping, he looked up. Mael smiled.

Christian crept into the room and Mael nodded to let Christian know everything was all right before he turned his attention back to Taylor. He let go of the tension with the first signs of returning life from Taylor. In a fraction of a second, Mael's mind blanketed over Taylor's to insure the new vampire would remain calm.

Because Taylor's senses couldn't handle sensory overload, the room remained very low lit. Anything of a bright color, or glaring white, had been temporarily removed, and the colors were in muted shades of grey. No sounds breached the walls.

When Taylor's eyes opened, Mael stood beside the bed. The barely restrained beast of Taylor's hunger struggled against the barrier Mael had formed around it. "We're here, Taylor. Everything is all right, and you're safe."

"Hungry."

Though Mael kept much in restraint for Taylor, it was still what the newly turned vampire's mind focused on. He knew every one of the boy's senses was zoomed in on the scents surrounding him. Looking to Mael, Cian settled down on the bed beside Taylor.

"Go ahead, Cian. You should feed him first."

Cian pulled Taylor close. Lying on his side, the angel bared his throat. The strike was visibly painful and quick. Cian tried to keep his gaze on Mael, but with every sharp pull from Taylor, it became increasingly more difficult. Christian chuckled as he sat on the other side of the bed. Mael settled beside them, resting his hand on Cian's hip. The four of them were their own form of a family now, though it was a definition most mortals wouldn't understand it all.

"Thank Michael that I'm an angel," Cian said silently to Mael.

"His body needs more blood than normal to ensure he survives."

Cian threaded his fingers through Taylor's hair as he relaxed against their son. "Thank you, Mael. Thank you so much." A few moments later, Cian urged Taylor to stop feeding, petting Taylor's hair as he rolled onto his back.

"I need to thank you as well, my angel."

When a feral growl sounded from Taylor, Mael laid a hand on him to strengthen the calming effect. The sound died off as Taylor licked his lips, but the hunger remained. Christian moved closer to Taylor when Mael nodded to him. A strong arm encircled Taylor, drawing him to sit up. As Christian bared his throat, Taylor's fangs buried in his skin. Christian gasped softly.

"How long will he have to feed like this before the initial hunger pains are gone?" Cian asked Mael.

"Once his body has enough blood, it will slow. For the next few days, it will be stronger than normal, but it won't be as bad as this."

"Shit," Christian muttered as he closed his eyes. The deep growls from Taylor were a clear indication the need for blood overrode everything else to him.

Smirking, Mael eyed Christian. "Now you know what you were like."

Cian just laughed, shaking his head at the two of them. "If I'm needed, let me know."

When Taylor had taken all Christian could allow him, Christian tried to pull away. Taylor's arms slid around him in an iron grip. Mael took hold of Taylor's shoulder. "Enough, child."

Taylor let go of Christian, and Christian fell back and made a valiant effort not to appear too afraid. Taylor, as a newly risen vampire, had the strength to drain him. When Taylor started growling again, Mael's attention returned to him and he held his arm out for his son to come to him. Crawling across the bed, Taylor held Mael's gaze for a moment before bending to sink his teeth into Mael's neck. His fingers clutched Mael's biceps, the sucking at Mael's throat strong.

Cian watched Mael in silence, his tongue sliding across his lips absently. Since Taylor had taken the formula, they hadn't had time to get much more than a kiss from each other. Mael tracked the signature power of his own blood through Taylor. He caught and held Cian's gaze as he stroked over Taylor's hair. The complete feeling of their unity gave Mael a strong sense of calm and peace. Christian slid up behind Mael and sank his fangs into the other side of Mael's throat. The draw from Christian wasn't heavy, and the act was an affirmation of family, done on pure instinct.

"Thank Michael I am an elder."

Giving Mael a wide but hardly angelic grin, Cian said, "I'll wait to attack you until later. Our boys have apparently staked their claim for the time being."

Mael's mind blanketed both of his children in the secure haven they both needed. All of it was part of who and what he was. Something he took very seriously. Both of his hands were occupied with Taylor and Christian; otherwise he would have reached for his angel.

With a chuckle, Mael murmured in a low voice, "Welcome to the world of children taking priority."

When Taylor and Christian had taken what they needed from him, both of them stopped feeding. Mael let go of them. Christian settled back on his knees, flashing Taylor a grin as a gleam of rational thought returned to the poor kid's brain.

Crooking his finger, Cian beckoned Mael over to him, even as Taylor turned and settled down beside him, hand resting on Cian's chest. Cian covered it with his other hand, curling his fingers tight around Taylor's. For the most part, Taylor remained silent, seemingly content where he was for the time being.

Mael leaned over Taylor to get to his angel. Dropping a quick kiss to Cian's lips, he whispered against them, "We'll never get a moment's peace; you know that, don't you?"

Cian let out a low growl and slid the fingers of his free hand through Mael's hair, tugging Mael back down for a real kiss. When he was satisfied, he let Mael go and smiled. "I know, but it's worth it."

Taylor grumbled and nestled closer. "Hey, now. I'm not that bad." His voice was a little rough from several days of disuse.

Mael agreed it was very much worth it. Hand against Taylor's side, he lightly pinched, chuckling. "Wait until you have one of your own."

Christian crept out of the bed, headed for the door, and let himself out.

"He's jealous." Cian looked up at Mael.

"He is uncertain he has any place in this. We'll get everything settled, Cian."

Cian lost a touch of his smile then. "He has a very big part in this." When Taylor dozed off, Cian managed to slide out from under him and reached out for Mael. "Please. A kiss, you feed me, I feed you, anything."

They could only do their best to show Christian he did have a part in this. Mael knew it. At his angel's 'request', he took hold of Cian's hand and pulled him close. "You are hungry, too, my angel." Since Mael had talked Cornelius into concocting him a potion to temporarily strengthen the power of his own blood, he had plenty to spare.

"Been hungry," Cian murmured, fingers sliding through Mael's hair. "Didn't want to take any when they needed you, too." His tongue pushed into Mael's mouth, the kiss soft but hungry. *"But I need you so much."*

If he hadn't have been so intent on Taylor, Mael would have noticed his angel's growing hunger. A small wound opened at the side of his throat, leaving a small trail of blood dripping down his skin. Cian moved swiftly, mouth covering the wound as he began to drink. He fisted his hands in Mael's hair until it was near painful. The flow of blood increased.

"Feed, my angel. Take as much as you need."

Mael tangled his fingers in the long, blonde hair, encouraging Cian. Growling against Mael's throat, Cian pushed Mael onto his back, crawling on top of him without stopping. As Cian fed, Mael relaxed beneath him. He opened himself completely, drawing Cian in and surrounding the sorcerer with his own deep well of inner peace.

Chapter Seventeen

Should his loyalty be to his grandfather? If one considered the amount of time and energy Nigel had devoted to raise Christian, the answer would be yes. The man might present the appearance of a cold fish, but no one doubted his devotion to his family. As the prince of Rome, he was stern, but fair. However, his Achilles' heel was his lineage; an obsession Christian never knew would drive him so far over the edge. He loved Nigel, had admired him from the first time they'd met. But how could Nigel expect Christian to agree with the destruction of his own father?

Christian was torn. He loved Mael, and he didn't doubt Mael's love for him. His father had taken great care to insure Christian understood its depths. A niggling doubt reminded him Nigel could kill them both with ease. He was powerless to stop the man.

Frightened for Mael and himself, Christian slumped against the wall behind him and slid to the floor. There wasn't a damn thing he could do, and he hated his own helplessness. He allowed himself to hate his own grandfather for the first time. Why did Nigel even fucking care what Mael did? Fuck Nigel's precious bloodlines. It wasn't worth the man's son.

"By the way, dad, Nigel is going to knock your ass out and drain you." He wanted to warn Mael, but what good would it do? Would Mael even believe him? Christian had no proof and had to admit the accusation sounded unlikely. Even with Nigel having fits about Cian and Taylor, nobody would think Nigel had gone off the deep end this bad.

To compact and hide everything deep inside him required concentration and expenditure of power. It wasn't beyond his abilities to appear as light-hearted and easy going as he did under normal circumstances. There was only place one he could go where it would all go away, if only for a short time. He got up and went to find Taylor.

* * *

A week had passed since Taylor's turning, and although he'd be isolated from everyone else for several months, he could practice his powers safely in one of the private rooms. He stood in the middle of the sparsely furnished area and focused on the pale blue light. Hands cupped, he willed it to grow. The light flickered and expanded until the blue nearly turned pure white. The sphere lit up the entire room better than any light bulb ever could. When Christian entered, he seemed startled. He stopped, one brow raised, and watched Taylor. Taylor flashed him a quick grin, then returned his attention to the sphere.

"I just learned how to do it," he said, manipulating the ball with his fingertips. He stretched it out until it became nothing but a mist. It felt warm and alive against his skin. "Wanna touch it?"

"You sure?" Christian eyed Taylor, just a touch wary.

"It's perfectly safe," Taylor chuckled. "It's the harmless version of the magic Cian uses. His is a lot stronger, and potentially more deadly." He took Christian's right hand and held it to the mist, his own beneath Christian's. "See? Kind of feels like a weird cross between spiderweb and cotton candy."

"It's about as odd as some of the stuff Corny does," Christian laughed. "How much magic will you be able to do?"

"At least my magic doesn't stink up the whole damn palace." Taylor willed the light to slip softly between Christian's fingers, then into his own palm below where it faded. "Learning Cian's magic isn't easy. There's nothing to read or memorize, so it takes a lot longer. He said I'll eventually learn everything he knows."

"That will make you powerful." Christian tilted his head, studying Taylor. There was a gleam of something resembling fascination in his eyes before he blinked. "Between your abilities from Mael and Cian, there shouldn't be much you have to worry about."

Taylor smiled. "I wouldn't say that, exactly. It'll take a long time for me to get anywhere near Cian's level. He's had over three thousand years of practice."

"Yeah, some of it will take a while, but you'll have abilities none of the rest of us have. It'll give you a certain advantage at some point." He turned his hand and took hold of Taylor's. "Anything else?"

For a moment, Taylor just stared at their linked fingers. He'd hoped that turning would ease the attraction, but he'd discovered it only deepened it. Feeding from Christian hadn't helped matters. The man was in his blood now. Taylor opened his mouth to respond, but a sharp pain shot up his spine. He hissed and rolled his shoulders.

"That was weird..." Shrugging it off, he started for the door, Christian's hand still in his. Just as he reached for the door handle, fire shot through him. He braced himself against the wall, stunned.

"What's wrong?"

"Get Cian." It was all Taylor could get out before he hit the floor. He felt as if his entire back was on fire, and he swore the bones shifted. Cian had warned him it would hurt.

Shadows gathered around Christian, and he disappeared within them. No more than a moment later, the black mass returned and both Christian and Cian stepped into the room.

Cian crouched down and tore Taylor's shirt off. "Breathe through it." His fingers smoothed along Taylor's back, and a second later, the skin split.

"Fuck!" Taylor threw his head back and shouted as another wound opened. He growled through the pain, shaking all over.

"The pain won't last," Cian said. "Deep breath, grit your teeth if you have to."

It was all the warning Taylor had before the blinding pain shot through him. He bit his lower lip, drawing blood, as his wings began to emerge. Cian helped, coaxing each one out.

Frozen, Christian watched. An almost imperceptible shiver ran through him the moment blood scented the air. Panting, Taylor caught only a cursory glance. Then the pain abruptly subsided and he gasped. Two large wings fanned out behind him, as brilliant blue as Cian's. Cian smoothed the bloodied feathers.

"It's over," Cian said. Even as he spoke, Taylor felt the wounds close, leaving the places where his wings connected to his shoulder blades completely seamless. "Be gentle with them. They're still new and somewhat fragile."

Taylor finally regained his senses and blinked. "Fuck, that hurt."

Christian crouched down beside Taylor, laying a hand on his arm for comfort. His gaze shifted between Taylor's face and the wings, then fixated on the wings. "They're fucking gorgeous."

Though he felt like he'd been through hell and back, Taylor smiled over at Christian. "Yeah?"

"Yeah. Just like you." Hand remaining on Taylor, Christian looked up at Cian. "That shit won't hurt anymore, will it?"

Cian smiled. "No. He should be fine, though I recommend a shower." He stood up. "Thank you for coming to get me, Christian." With a bow, he left them alone once more.

"Do you really think that?"

"Think what? You mean the part about how you and your wings are gorgeous? Well, yeah. Don't you ever look in the mirror?"

Taylor grew warm. "I don't make a habit of it, no. I've just never had anyone say that."

Christian's lips twitched, but he didn't laugh as he helped Taylor up. "Take a shower, and while you're at it, take a good look in the mirror. I'll wait for you out here."

Taylor smirked. "Yes, sir."

Christian tugged at the torn shirt to help get it off, then slapped Taylor's ass. "Go."

A groan escaped before Taylor could bite it back. "Tease."

A gentle shove helped Taylor on his way. "Only because you let me."

"I'd let you do a lot more," Taylor muttered before opening the door.

* * *

Christian poured a glass of blood for himself. He needed it since he'd gotten more than a whiff of Taylor's. There was a special characteristic to it Christian couldn't place. The scent of it intrigued him far more than anyone else's, except for his father's. It wouldn't do him any good at all to crave Taylor. Cian and Mael both would have incredible fits if they caught even a whiff of anything. With a sigh, he stared at the ruby red liquid in his glass. His life was hell enough as it was.

Half an hour later, Taylor walked into Christian's room, hair still damp and clinging to his bare chest. "I needed that."

An approving gaze roamed over Taylor before Christian could help himself. "You look a lot better. You gonna show off your wings?"

Smiling, Taylor unfurled his wings. The brilliant blue feathers reflected the light and shimmered when Taylor moved them slowly. "Cian showed me how to let them out once I finished my shower."

"Makes me wish I had a pair." Christian took a healthy swallow of the blood. "Can I touch?"

"Of course."

Eyes fixed on the wings, he set the glass aside and forgot about it. He got up and stood behind Taylor. "Wow, they are so beautiful, Taylor. Have you gotten a good look at them?"

Taylor shivered the slightest bit. "Only a little..."

"Must be strange and awesome to have wings." A light touch followed the words. The feathers begged to be touch. Yet he was hesitant, almost afraid of hurting Taylor.

Taylor gasped softly. "Wow."

"Wow." Christian echoed the word, momentarily lost in the softness. It took a moment longer for him to catch the faintest hint of arousal. "Oh, *wow*."

"Chris." Taylor grasped Christian's hand gently. "Any more, and I'll be on my knees..."

"Oh, hey, sorry. Not a good idea, huh?"

Taylor's laugh was shaky. "Depends on who you're asking."

"Better put those things away before they get you into trouble." It took a concerted effort to appear as cheerful and carefree as he did most of the time with Taylor. No good would come of their attraction to each other. Not a good idea at all.

Taylor hid them once more. "Hey." He caught Christian, one hand softly cupping the side of Christian's face. "It's okay."

For an instant, just for an instant, Christian pressed into the touch. He murmured, "I wonder if it's the angel blood that keeps you warm."

"Maybe it is." Taylor's thumb brushed lightly along Christian's lower lip. "Maybe it's something else entirely."

Christian shivered. He couldn't think past the sensation of Taylor so close to him. The urge to get even closer was nigh impossible to resist. What the hell was wrong with him? Was there anything wrong with wanting a kiss? Taylor closed the distance before either of them could come to their senses. Eyes drifting shut, he pressed a soft kiss to Christian's lips, then teased them apart with his tongue.

"Fuck," Christian whispered before he was silenced into opening for Taylor. He sensed something behind this kiss but couldn't think enough to question it. There was no sense of urgency between them, but there was undeniably *something*.

Taylor's tongue grazed one of Christian's fangs, the slightest bit of blood flavoring the kiss. Christian growled softly. He'd thought Taylor's blood would be good, but he wasn't prepared for just how good. With considerable will power, Christian stopped himself from taking more and pulled back from Taylor.

Looking more than a bit dazed, Taylor licked his own lips. "You have no idea how long I've waited for that. If I stay in this room any longer, though, I'm afraid I'll want far more than you might be willing to give."

"That's the stupidest thing either of us have ever done. Under normal circumstances, it'd be okay, but it's not normal circumstances."

Taylor smiled and reached for the door. Just before he opened it, he looked back at Christian. "I don't regret it, even if I never get it again."

Christian didn't regret it either. His regret was because there could be nothing between them.

* * *

Cian blew out a breath and walked into the office. "That brought back some intense memories," he said after he closed the door. He sprawled out in one of the chairs, the energy nearly sapped out of him.

"What was the problem?" Mael looked up from the paperwork strewn across his desk. He placed the papers in his hand into an open folder, then gave his full attention to Cian.

"Taylor's wings emerged. It's a painful, bloody event." Cian shivered. "Reminded me of my own."

"Is he all right now? Perhaps I should have gone with you. I could have helped, or at least anesthetized the pain."

Cian smiled. "He's okay. Christian stayed with him."

"Christian can do the same thing. I believe those two are adjusting well to the circumstances, and Taylor is doing excellent with the change."

Chuckling softly, Cian toyed with the arm of his chair. "I think we can thank Christian for Taylor's handling of everything."

"He will make a good father one day, if he could be convinced of it. The boy is as stubborn as I am at times."

"I wouldn't argue that," Cian said quietly, "especially when someone loves him."

"Is there something I should know?"

"Taylor's fallen in love with Christian."

"Is that so wise?"

"Ultimately, it is up to them to decide, I think." Cian stood and sat on the corner of the desk nearest Mael. "To be honest, he was afraid to tell you. He didn't have to tell me. You know I have the ability to see things like this."

"There's no reason to be afraid to tell me anything."

Cian smiled and ran the fingers of one hand through Mael's hair. "Don't be so worried, cariad. Taylor isn't afraid of you. In fact, I think he idolizes you. He's more concerned with how you'd react because Christian is your son, too."

Mael relaxed. "Years ago, it would have bothered me, and right now, it would be hard to explain but Christian needs it from me."

"You're a wonderful father, Mael. You might not be the most... affectionate man at times," Cian said with a teasing smile, "but your love and devotion are clear."

Mael reached out and drew Cian onto his lap. "That affection part is something I have to work on. It's been engrained that unseemly displays are not acceptable public behavior. In private, it's different, regardless of what Nigel ever said."

"I don't know what the outcome between Taylor and Christian will be, but I do know they've grown close. Taylor understands that Christian may not feel the same, and he accepts the possibility. But I speak from experience when I say love can change a man. You are proof of that."

"I have a few doubts about those two, but will allow them to make their own mistakes. Things will be fair more complicated than Taylor might understand at first. However, I am proof of what an angel can do."

Cian chuckled. "Wanna take bets on how long it'll be before Christian gets a taste of angel blood?"

"Why?"

With a knowing grin, Cian brushed his thumb over Mael's lips, coaxing them open. Then he touched the tip of one of Mael's fangs. A droplet of blood landed on Mael's tongue. "Because angel blood is stronger than a human's, and far more addictive."

Mael licked Cian's fingertip before releasing it. "Are you trying to tell me something?"

"Nothing concrete, but I have the feeling things are going to change for them soon. Only time will tell how they handle it."

"I doubt there's much either of us can do." Mael took hold of Cian's hand and drew it back to his lips. "We have lessons to arrange for Taylor. Perhaps we can focus on that."

Cian traced Mael's lower lip, slipping his fingers into the prince's mouth to brush the fangs. "Like... ?"

"You are trying to distract me, love. You'll have to take care of the angel things he is supposed to learn. I need to take care of his blood abilities, have Cornelius teach him some things, and make sure our son knows his history, fighting skills, how to run a city. It is a very long list."

"Spoil sport." Cian smirked. "He's been learning angelic magic, and he now knows how to bring out and hide his wings. He can conjure the spheres without much trouble, though he's a long way from using the fire versions of them like I did."

"We'll have to coordinate his lessons. He has a lot more to learn than most."

"What are the chances he inherited your rather deadly gold allergy?"

"Christian doesn't have it, so it's not likely Taylor will."

"That makes me feel a bit better," Cian said. "I want him to learn to fight with a sword, as well as with his vampire abilities. My sword has gold in the grip and pommel."

"It was something I had when I was alive. It has never transferred to any of my children, so no worries. He won't be able to wield Michael's sword, though, not with his vampire blood."

Chapter Eighteen

Christian saw Nigel inside Mael's study when he opened the door. He stopped in surprise. His grandfather said nothing to him. He knew what Nigel was up to when the man opened Mael's decanter of brandy. Christian saw only a flash of the vial in Nigel's hand.

A pleased smile curled Nigel's lips, and Christian wanted to stop him, wanted to protest. There was no way his grandfather would listen to him, and it kept Christian silent.

His father hadn't done anything wrong, but Nigel had the right to exact punishment for the crimes he perceived Mael to have committed. Torn between the two, Christian remained motionless as Nigel disappeared into the darkness his grandfather had summoned.

As if all the life drained from him, Christian dropped to the floor, staring blindly into the fireplace.

* * *

Mael entered the room and watched his son in silence. Settling into his chair, he asked, "You wanted to talk to me, Christian?"

"I think maybe I should return to Nigel. If anything, it'll make things easier for you."

Mael kept his sadness hidden. "No, it won't make anything any easier. You know I want more than anything for you to stay here. You are a part of my family, and you always will be. Are you sure about your decision?"

Christian gave him a pained smile. "There isn't any real reason for you to want me around. You have Cian and Taylor now."

Mael got up and crouched in front of his son. "Do you really believe I love you any less because of them? I won't stand in your way if you want to return to Nigel's home, but I want you to know when you go away, it leaves an empty space inside me. You are my son. Nothing will ever change that as far as I'm concerned."

"I'm sorry, Father." For what, Christian didn't say, but he seemed near tears.

Mael straightened slowly with a nod. "Some times you don't realize just how much I can forgive, my child, especially from you."

Christian stood as quickly as he could. "I have to go."

"All right."

Mael picked up his glass of brandy. Halfway to the door, Christian glanced back, painful indecision on his face. He went to turn away from Mael, but before he touched the door, he appeared to change his mind. In one swift motion, he knocked the glass out of Mael's hand before he broke down. Mael wasn't surprised. He knew far more than Christian understood. Gathering his son to him, he held him in a tight embrace.

The words poured from Christian in between his sobs. "He wants to kill you... tried to get rid of Cian. I'm so sorry, Father."

"I know. But I knew in my heart, you wouldn't be able to follow through with it." Mael smoothed his hand gently over Christian's hair. He had more faith in his son than Christian had in himself. "I also know who is behind everything." Christian pulled away from Mael, fear in his eyes.

"Useless whelp!" Nigel stepped out of the darkness and grabbed Christian's arm. He yanked Christian up and delivered a hard slap to his face. "You'll rue the day you broke my trust."

Mael shot to his feet, shoving his Father backward with one hand. "Do *not* touch my son again, Nigel."

"You don't dictate my behavior, Mael, nor will you ever do so. I have no use for your useless offspring or you at this point." With a negligent wave of Nigel's hand, he sent a crackling burst of energy at Christian.

Mael intercepted the attack and Christian screamed, "No, father!"

The scorching power burst into flames over Mael's body. He used a small portion of his energy to extinguish the flames, then sent Nigel flying back against the wall. Nigel remained pinned by Mael's power, and Mael advanced on his father in a blind rage.

"Get out or I will kill you!"

No sooner had the words left Mael's mouth, did the door fly open, the force nearly snapping the wooden door from its metal hinges. Taylor skirted behind Cian and ran to Christian's side, tugging his arm to get him well out of harm's way. The wrath of Heaven had nothing on the fire blazing in Cian's eyes. His wings unfurled. Taylor pulled Christian farther into a corner. Mael grabbed Nigel's neck. His nails lengthened into talons, digging into his father's flesh.

With a sneer, Nigel wrapped his fingers around Mael's throat, but his attention was distracted. A hate-filled gaze focused on Taylor. "Abomination!"

A surge of power flared from Nigel's hand. Before the lethal power could envelope Taylor, Christian shoved Taylor out of the way. Encased in the shaft of pure sunlight, Christian screamed, the light searing him. An explosive sound filled the room as Nigel tried to bring Mael to his knees, but he refused to let go. Only the sound of his son's scream cut through to Mael.

"Cian, my son!"

Before the words had completely left Mael's mouth, Cian had Christian's arm in a death grip, tearing him away from the sunlight. Cian murmured something and started the slow healing process. "Our sons," he growled, advancing on Nigel and Mael.

Mael shielded Taylor and Christian within the safety of the shadows. However, the enormous amount of power he used weakened him. In retaliation, he began feeding off Nigel's blood to fuel himself. With a roar of anger, Nigel broke free, and a powerful blow to Mael's head forced him backward.

Cian caught Mael and shoved the prince behind him. *"Shield yourself."*

The moment Mael did so, Cian rushed Nigel, lifting him off of the floor and holding him against the wall. Blue flames erupted around Cian and crawled up his arms, licking at Nigel's body. The chanted prayer thundered within the room, bouncing off of the walls around them, each word containing power, building in strength as Cian spoke.

Unable to fully combat Cian's power, Nigel shrieked when his skin caught fire. Another powerful blow knocked Cian's hands off of him, and in a blur, Nigel went to the other side of the room. The blue fire continued crawling over his skin even as he tried to put it out. Anger twisted his features and he snarled at both of them.

A purely murderous look contorted Mael's face. Right now, he would be satisfied with nothing less than Nigel's death. But before Mael could advance on him, Diocourides entered the room. Without a word said, the sheer force of his power lifted Nigel and suspended him in midair.

"Enough." The word, though softly spoken, was more than enough to give both Nigel and Mael pause. They had no choice but to obey. "Return to your home now, Nigel, or I will insure your destruction without thought."

Mael went to Cian, the damage barely healing. Enfolding them both in his wings, Cian pressed Mael to his neck. "Drink until you've had your fill. You cannot weaken me right now."

Shadows swallowed Nigel before Diocourides turned to Cian. "Nigel won't like what happens to him if this nonsense continues." After he made the promise, he left them alone.

Cian stroked Mael's hair softly, holding him tightly. As Mael fed, the powerful angelic blood rushed through him. A quiet blanket of calm engulfed both of them in an effort to still the erratic energy pulsing through Cian. The black skin on Mael's body sloughed away, revealing new skin beneath. When he'd finally taken what he need, Mael healed the wounds.

The shadows protecting Taylor and Christian released them and left them standing not too far away from their fathers. Mael heard Taylor whisper something about the kitchen, then both sons left the office. The moment the door closed, Cian shoved Mael against the wall, crushing their mouths together. The kiss was more desperation than anything else, the last of Cian's fear and rage dissolving. A sharp nick from Mael's fangs cut Cian's bottom lip and his blood tinged their kiss.

The kiss eased and Cian rested his forehead to Mael's, eyes closed. "I'm so afraid to let you go," he ground out, voice deep and rasping. Pulses of energy still radiated through him, more subdued but still there.

"It's all right, my angel." No doubt Diocourides would take care of his Father, and there was no way Nigel could refuse to obey their creator.

"If anyone lays another finger on you, Taylor, or Christian, I will kill them." The words were more growled than said, Cian shuddering with the vehemence behind them.

Mael couldn't help but chuckle. "Likewise. Not even Diocourides would be able to stop me. Somehow I think Nigel isn't up to testing our creator, though."

"Love you," Cian whispered. "I love them, Mael."

Mael understood Cian had finally taken Christian into his heart, and he was grateful for that. "I love you, too. There are many things about Christian you don't understand. A great deal I'm uncertain of telling, but I know him so well. Eventually he will come to you to confess everything."

"I can't promise that I won't be angry, but rest assured, it will not change what I feel. An angel does not give love freely, and we never take it back."

"Nigel used Christian to get rid of you. When it failed, Nigel planned to reclaim my blood, and Christian knew his plans. I wasn't sure precisely what Christian would do. I waited to give him a chance to make his own decision. I knew in my heart that I could have faith in him."

Cian remained quiet, then took a deep breath. "I trust your judgment above all others, Mael. Your faith and love for

Christian were Nigel's undoing. Now? We have two children and you are still with me. For that, I am blessed."

* * *

Taylor waited until they were alone in the kitchen before saying a word. "What the hell?" He gestured helplessly in the general direction of Mael's office where all hell had broken loose only moments ago. "Christian?"

Christian didn't say anything. He took his time opening the fridge door. He got out a small bottle and heated it under the tap. Taylor caught his hand, forcing Christian to look at him.

"You were there. What happened?"

"My grandfather attacked me and my father." Christian's shoulders drooped in defeat and he stared down at the bottle in his hand. "It all failed. I failed."

Taylor took the bottle and set it on the counter. Then he cupped Christian's face. "What failed, Christian?"

All life drained from Christian's face. He opened his mouth to say something, but didn't utter a sound. He just shook his head, clearly still in shock. Realization began to sink into Taylor.

"Please," Taylor whispered. "Tell me this wasn't... Oh, God." He lowered his hands and backed away. "Christian, what did you do?

Christian grabbed the bottle once more, opened it, and drained it. When he spoke, each word was uttered in a precise monotone. "I betrayed my father and Cian. Grandfather tried to kill them, then tried to kill me for failing him."

Taylor grabbed Christian's shoulders. "How could you? I loved you! I would have given you my soul!"

Christian stared at Taylor. He made no move to protect himself or even quiet Taylor. If anything, he appeared even deader. "You made a poor choice."

"No fucking wonder you pushed me away. I would have done anything for you, Christian. *Anything.*" Taylor stepped backward, every inch making the pain worse. "And all I got for my love is betrayal?"

A pained smile crossed Christian's lips. The gesture only strengthened the bleakness in his eyes, and emptiness echoed in his voice. "I'm sorry, Taylor. I never meant to hurt you."

"Did you ever, even once..." Taylor looked away and swallowed past the lump in his throat.

"Would you believe anything I said?"

"What could you possibly say that would make it feel less like my heart's been torn out?"

"I'm sorry." Darkness gathered around Christian and he disappeared within it.

* * *

Something was wrong. Echoes of distress resounded within the ever-present darkness. Mael stiffened. His son. He knew it was Christian, blind, lost, and alone within the black void. Before he could react, the familiar sense of his child filled him as Christian sought sanctuary. Mael cursed himself, anger rising the moment he realized how badly Christian had been damaged. Cian gave him an alarmed look.

"I need to get to Christian."

At the angel's nod, Mael disappeared into the gathering blackness. Shadowy creatures hovered around Christian's crumpled body, and Mael motioned them away before he picked his son up. Agitated, Christian's guardians twined to the motionless form and around Mael as well. His rage at himself rose to dangerous levels, but he kept Christian shielded in the safe harbor his son needed. Everything Mael should have done hammered at him and left him guilt-ridden. How had he failed so badly?

* * *

"I should've stayed." Taylor leaned against the bedpost. The softness of the bed offered no comfort. "I should never have come here."

"You would have died on the streets if you hadn't."

Taylor didn't look up. "I wouldn't have fallen in love."

Cian sat down beside him. "Is it such a strong price to pay?"

Was it? Taylor had no idea. Christian was gone, and all Taylor could see anymore was the devastation on Christian's face. "I don't know. Maybe if I hadn't..." He swallowed and didn't bother to wipe away the tears this time.

"Taylor." Cian's arms and wings encircled him and Taylor struggled not to break down. Again. "You aren't to blame. Christian isn't to blame. Nigel is gone, but Mael and I are equally at fault."

"I miss him," Taylor whispered.

Cian was silent for a moment, then said, "So do I."

Chapter Nineteen

"Well, well..."

Cian froze and watched as a group of about ten vampires circled him. Although he could take them on, it would be a rough fight. "What do you want?"

One of them sneered. "It seems you're a thorn in someone's side. And the rumors about you..." The vampire shook his head and tsked.

Eyes narrowing, Cian glanced around. The group surrounded him, and he thanked the heavens above that no mortals were out this late. "I'm good at being a nuisance." He smiled slowly. "I'm also a lot more than I seem."

The vampires lunged at him all at once. Fangs and nails tore at him, but he never allowed them to hold on for long.

"Get a fucking hold of him, you bastards!"

They circled Cian, pushing him toward the warehouse behind him. A large door off to the side opened, and a few other vampires inside became visible. A clawed hand sliced at Cian, one of the vampires growling menacingly. Another group blocked the left to keep Cian from straying away from the warehouse.

Another cut came from behind and Cian whirled around. Several more followed, the vampires—now nearly fifteen in number—threatening to completely overtake him. It took six of them, but the vampires managed to seize him. Before Cian could retaliate, his attackers shoved him into the warehouse. He spun and finally gained purchase, blue fire igniting one of the vampires and turning her to dust.

As a collective whole, the others froze. Several savage growls echoed in the cavernous room full of broken, rusted equipment. One of the vampires looked up toward an unseen presence.

"Stop playing around." Nigel stepped into the dim overhead light. "Kill him, whatever it takes."

Weapons appeared as three men and two women advanced on Cian. A gunshot, then another, rang out and the bullets hit Cian square in the chest. One of the men smirked as five others decided to join in on the fun. Each shot robbed him of breath, but it was nothing compared to the pure fury that raged through him the second he saw Nigel.

When it was apparent the bullets didn't harm him, one of the vampires threw her gun to the floor. "What the fuck are you?" she shouted. The others stopped firing, all staring as the wounds healed, one by one.

"Nothing you can ever kill," Cian answered. Before anyone could do as much as blink, he hurled a sphere of blue light at a small cluster of vampires. They all shrieked, skin burning with blue flames before, one by one, they fell to piles of ash.

"Looks like things are getting out of hand." Apollonius stepped from the darkness near Nigel and drew someone with him. An aura of black energy swarmed right above his head, visible in the light.

What sounded like another voice came from Apollonius. "Oh, this is too delicious. He's not ordinary at all. I didn't expect this, but I can work with it." Apollonius pulled the other man with him into the light. In the same odd voice, he said, "I believe you two know each other."

"Josh." The sight of Diocourides' companion did what the bullets could not. Cian froze. Josh struggled, tendrils of shadows writhing in wild strands about him. Whenever one tried to get near Apollonius, it withered away. "What have you done to him?"

Apollonius shrugged. "Call him... a bargaining chip."

Cian started for them, but one touch of a blade to Josh's throat stopped him cold. "What do you want?"

Nigel grabbed hold of Josh's other arm. "What in the name of the sacred gods are you doing? How dare you lay a hand on Diocourides' companion!" He raised the cane in his other hand, and with a press of his thumb, a knife protruded from the end. Before Apollonius could stop him, Nigel slashed at him. An enormous wave of energy erupted from Nigel, and the room began to heat to a near uncomfortable level. "You stupid fool, you told me nothing of this! You have no right to touch this boy!"

Apollonius laughed, the sound sending a chill down Cian's spine. "Do you think I care of such things?" He looked from Nigel to Cian. "And what of you," he asked in the odd voice as before. "You are not what you seem."

Massive blue wings fanned out, and the vampires scurried away from Cian. "I will be the one to insure your death should you harm Josh."

"An angel. Far more interesting than an ordinary sorcerer. Oh, and just a warning to you, I'm impossible to kill."

Black flames sprang from Nigel and covered Apollonius. None touched Josh, who had stopped struggling and eyed them all, terrified. Through the fire, Apollonius laughed.

"You have nothing on me, Nigel. No power and no chance. Leave while you can."

"Not without this child!" Using both hands, Nigel tried to get Josh away from the mad man. With a snarl of anger, Apollonius held out his hand, and a mist poured from it to envelop Nigel. An unearthly scream echoed in the vast room as the mist turned blood red. Nigel dropped to the floor still screaming.

"It'll take him a while to get all that blood back.

Cian rushed to Nigel's side the second the mist evaporated. He cut his own wrist and pressed it Nigel's lips, but the vampire slipped into a blood coma. "What do you want!" he shouted, rage fueling the urge to tear Apollonius apart. "Release Josh—keep me!"

"Since you are a far more interesting specimen, I just might grant your wish. You behave for the time being until I have you safely stowed away, and I won't harm a hair on this pretty young man's head. How's that?"

"Done." Cian withdrew and sat back on his heels. Wings hidden, he allowed the vampires to bind him. "What about Nigel?"

Another arrogant smirk graced Apollonius' face. "Someone will find him sooner or later. Whenever I decide to send out a message. I'm sure his boy will take tender, loving care of him. Don't you agree?" Apollonius and Josh headed outside. Two vampires ushered Cian to follow them. Apollonius gave him a speculative look when they stopped beside two limos. "I'm really surprised you haven't asked what I am. So do you know or are you guessing?"

"I know." Cian glared at him. "I may not know who, but I know a god when I feel one."

Apollonius grinned, then ushered Josh to the other limo. Cian attempted to reach out to Mael. Whatever god resided within Apollonius prevented any form of communication. It left only one option.

"My Lord, please hear me out," he thought. *"The Romanorum has been betrayed, and I gave up resistance to keep Diocourides' companion from harm. Please, go to Rome—to Mael and Diocourides."*

A few minutes later, Apollonius returned. He sat in back with Cian, and the dark mass, in graduated shades of black and gray, pulsed around the vampire. "You were right about the god part. I'm an Egyptian, from long ago. If it would help, the name is Seth. I'm a lot older than you by a few millennia if that's a better hint. Now just relax and enjoy the ride. You'll be with us for a while to come."

"Michael... he claims to be the Egyptian god, Seth. He's powerful enough to be what he says."

* * *

Cian's message came through, and the mere mention of Seth gave Michael plenty of reason to pause. Michael entered the palace in Rome and followed the sounds of commotion. Upon reaching a closed door, he threw it open to find Mael Black and another man, both looking like they were ready to rip someone to shreds.

"Mael. I've come with a warning from Cian."

Both men stared at him, then Mael asked, agitated, "Where is he?"

"Apollonius has betrayed the Romanorum. He is in league with an ancient Egyptian god named Seth." Michael looked to the other man, then back to Mael. "They have Cian... and Josh. Cian has relinquished all control to insure Josh's safety."

"Josh!" Fury erupted from the normal light-hearted, carefree Dio. "That bastard! It wasn't enough he tried kill off Xander, now he seeks revenge against me!"

"You know this creature, Diocourides?" Mael asked.

"Our kind had dealings with him when he tried to kill Osiris and his host, Xander, who dates the favored one of Prince Gabriel of San Diego. Seth failed in his attempt because of the interference of the first formula Nikolai, Gabriel, and the ghoul Adrian." Diocourides paced in furious steps, his face contorted in rage.

"Are there others we can contact, Diocourides?" Michael asked. "I can handle Seth, but this is a very delicate matter."

"We will have to. Not even I can deal with him alone." Before Dio even finished speaking, a portal of dark shadows appeared and two men stepped from it.

"You wished our presence, Diocourides?" A spiky-haired vampire bowed respectfully to Diocourides as the other, a slightly younger vampire with dark hair to his shoulders, bowed as well.

Mael stood beside Michael, obviously trying to hide how upset he was. He bowed to Nikolai and murmured, "Your Eminence" before he nodded to Gabriel.

"Nikolai, Gabriel, we have a serious problem."

"What can we do?" Gabriel asked. "I don't think I've ever seen you like this."

"I know Xander is still with you and Adrian, Gabriel. Can you summon him?" Dio asked as he continued pacing.

"If you wish him here, I'll call him."

Black eyes narrowed, Nikolai took in the extreme behavior of their ruler. "What's going on, Diocourides?"

Michael stepped in to answer. "Seth, a god I'm sure you've had dealings with before, has returned. He's in league with a vampire by the name of Apollonius to overthrow the Romanorum. They've taken two hostages: Josh and Cian."

"The bastard took my Josh and Prince Mael's companion, Cian. And I want them back." It took serious, visible effort for Dio to calm himself, but he managed.

"Shit," Gabriel muttered, just as another portal opened. His own companions, Adrian and Xander, stepped through.

"What's wrong?" Adrian asked right away. It wasn't hard to tell something bad was going on.

Gabriel filled them in. "Seth kidnapped Diocourides' companion as well as Prince Mael's. It sounds like he's trying to get back at all of us."

Xander didn't appear the least bit puzzled. An odd gold energy framed him, but it didn't obscure him from sight. "I'd be willing to bet the little fucker thought he could go after your kind without reprisals from the rest of us. Osiris agrees."

"I have a direct link to Cian that is unbreakable," Michael said. "Do we know where they might be headed?"

Gabriel looked to Xander. "Is there any way to trace them?"

"Easy enough." Xander closed his eyes and several moments of silence followed before he opened them again. "I saw a blonde man near Seth. They're both in a limo, talking. Or to be more accurate, Seth is bragging. The other one, a young boy, I believe, is in another car. Both are safe for the time being. I can sense Seth has no intention of harming them, yet."

"Will Horus and Anubis help us, Xander?"

"Yeah, they will, Gabriel. As will a few others. Seth's antics are getting to be a bit much for all of us."

All eyes turned to the doorway a split second later. Two men stood there, one wearing a silver mask over half of his face.

"Triarius, we have found Apollonius and know what we're dealing with now." Dio sat on his couch and invited Triarius to join him. He glanced over at Xander, "You have all the help the Romanorum has to offer. Let Anubis and Horus know as well." For the first time since he'd found out Josh had gone missing, Dio seemed relaxed.

"My help as well," Nikolai offered with a faint smile. "Seth needs to learn a lesson about interfering in our business."

"We'll be calling on everybody for help. It will take a few days to coordinate all of us and come up with a plan. I can keep tabs on Seth with no problem. And as I said, I don't sense he will hurt either of his hostages."

"You can handle Osiris, Anubis, and the other mummies, Xander. The rest of us will deal with the vampire forces," Gabriel said.

"I'm keeping communication open with Cian," Michael added. "Apparently Seth's magic has managed to block anything else. Mael, you know how to find me. I am at your disposal." With a bow, Michael left.

Triarius remained relatively silent while he and Lance joined Dio on the couch. It was Lance who spoke for them. "What do you need from us, Diocourides?"

"I am relying on Nikolai to take the lead on this. Lance, I need you to keep Triarius out of it." At Triarius' look of impending argument, Dio lifted a hand. "I need Apollonius intact. I know you're still dealing with the betrayal. Please don't fight me on this."

Triarius sighed. "As you wish, father."

Dio's gaze traveled over the others. "None of this goes beyond this room. Osiris, Anubis, and Horus have already proven to be our allies, and in return, we have agreed to keep their existence as secret as they wish. Am I understood?"

"We'll return to San Diego, and once Horus and Anubis join us, we'll return here, Diocourides. There are a few more contacts I need to make, too."

"Thank you, Xander. I know it's unusual for yours or mine to stir for the other, and I appreciate this alliance that has sprung up between us."

"You have Adrian to thank for that. If I didn't help, he'd have my head."

Xander laughed when Adrian said, "Damn straight."

The others departed in their own ways, leaving just Mael, Dio, Lance, and Triarius. Triarius appeared to be handling things much better than he had upon learning of Apollonius' initial treachery. Lance rubbed Triarius' shoulders.

All of a sudden, Mael staggered and reached out, groping for the wall. "My father. Something's wrong."

Before anybody could say a word, there was a knock at the door and it opened. "Forgive me for disturbing you, Diocourides. I believe this is important. It's for Prince Black."

Mael grabbed the note from Roberto and scanned it. "He's got my father."

"Go, Mael, and bring Nigel back here."

Without a word Mael followed Roberto out of the room.

Chapter Twenty

Diocourides sat in the middle of his sanctuary, crossed legged on the ground. The lulling murmur of an artificial waterfall provided a soothing backdrop to the rustling of the small animals around him. Overhead, soft fairy lights lit the garden with a white glow. The outer door of his office opened and several men came into the garden. One of them was cloaked, and the other two Dio recognized as Xander and Prince Gabriel.

"Grab whatever seat you want. This is just an informal meeting to make our plans.

"It's about time I met the illustrious Diocourides. My name is Anubis." The shrouded mummy inclined his head before he sat on the ground near Dio.

"Nice to see you again, Dio." Xander gave him a friendly wave before he made himself at home on one of the stone benches. Gabriel followed with a more formal greeting.

The door opened once more, and Mael joined them. A moment later, Michael followed. They both sat with the others.

"Good evening, Diocourides," Michael said, bowing his head.

"Evening, Michael." Dio winked at him. "No need for formality with me. You should know that better than most.

One eyebrow lifted and Michael smiled. "Perhaps you're correct."

Anubis spoke first. "Seth is next to impossible to destroy. At best, we destroy his host and disable him enough to keep him out of commission for a century or two."

"I can handle whatever is needed," Michael said. "Cian's sole focus will be Josh. With Josh safe, we can deal with Seth and his accomplice."

Mael didn't appear as if he liked the sound of Cian being in harm's way out of a sense of duty. Again. "Does Seth know how to kill an angel?"

Dio groaned. "Thank you for sharing that little tidbit with the group, Mael. I'm sure the information will go no further."

Mael blinked, then cursed softly under his breath. "Nerves."

Michael chuckled and patted the prince's shoulder. "Even we princes make mistakes, Mael."

"Seth can take out many creatures" Xander answered, "but as long as he's busy, he won't have time to worry about Josh or Cian."

Anubis stared, thoughtful, into the nearby pool of water. "I would suggest we remain in the background at first. If Seth believes all he is dealing with is a bunch of vampires, he'll be more easily ambushed."

Michael nodded. "I agree. However, it means I'll need to play least in sight. I've been in touch with Cian mentally. Seth knows what Cian is, which means he will most certainly know about me. I can keep watch on Cian and Josh until I'm needed."

"I think I can manage ample forces to occupy Seth. I will be there as well."

Both Gabriel and Mael looked alarmed, but Gabriel found his voice first. "Is that wise, Diocourides? If anything happens to you, it would create havoc in the Romanorum."

"Who best to protect my family?" It would do no good to argue with him, and a pointed look between the two vampires furthered his point.

Mael opened his mouth to protest, then shut it once again. He shook his head. "I don't like the idea, but I won't argue."

"I know, and I appreciate the concern, Mael," Dio said. "Between the gods present..." He glanced at Michael. "... it's going to take a significant amount of power to deal with Seth and his accomplice."

Michael smiled. "I am at your disposal."

"Ma'at and Thoth have chosen to join us. I know very well my brother won't expect us, which is why it's best if we don't reveal our presence too soon. It won't occur to him you've gained our aid, but it won't be easy to defeat him since he does have considerable magical ability on his side. If your vampires can distract him long enough, we'll have surprise on our side."

Anubis nodded. "I agree, Xander. Keeping him occupied will be the job of Diocourides' and his vampires."

"I've brought a large contingent of my elders secretly into the city, both first and second formulas to help. Do we know where Seth is?" Dio asked.

"Cian's last communication came about an hour ago," Michael said. "He knows they're still in Rome, but beyond that, he has no idea. Can one of you track Seth?"

"I know where he is." Xander smirked. "He's not even bothering to hide his signature. For the first time, my brother is making serious mistakes."

"Do we know who his host is?" Mael asked. "Apollonius will be easy enough to handle, I would think. He's third formula, and has considerably less power than any of us."

"He's a mortal named Curtis Woods, I believe," Anubis said. "He'll be easy enough to destroy, though Seth will make every effort to protect him. Seth has had him less than a year. After we destroyed his last host, Seth had to make due with what he had on hand. I heard he wasn't very happy about it."

Dio listened to all of them, then suggested, "I say we attack Seth in two nights' time. I can't hide the presence of my elders in the city for long. Soon rumors will spread, and we can't afford them."

"Agreed," Michael said.

"So do I." Mael nodded. "It gives them time to become complacent and possibly sloppy in their defenses.

"Than we are all agreed." Dio smiled in satisfaction. It was time to put an end to the bullshit, well past time.

* * *

"How is he?" Dio asked as he entered the bedroom.

"Still the same." Mael didn't get up from his position next to Nigel's side. Between the kidnapping of his angel and Nigel's state, Mael was looking more than a touch haggard.

The Prince of Rome remained in a magically-induced coma. Even though they had dealt with the blood loss Nigel had suffered, the vampire hadn't revived. Dio had been working with his most experienced magicians, and it would take a bit of time to come up with something to counter what Seth used on Nigel. "You need to rest, Mael. We know what we need to for your father, but it will take a bit of time to concoct." Before Mael could speak, Dio stalked over to him. He lifted his wrist to Mael's lips. "Drink and get some rest. You're going to need it tomorrow night. I'll take care of your father."

With a sigh, Mael gave in as he held Dio's wrist. He pierced the soft flesh and drank heavily. They both knew he needed the strength. Mael's worry had taken a great toll on him. Dio smoothed his other hand over the long dark hair. His blood was the strongest and would revitalize Mael. A good rest would help, too.

"Nigel will be fine, and we'll get Cian back, Mael."

An overwhelming sense of his true creator swelled within Mael, and the deeper he fed, the more he relaxed. Nigel was his father, but Diocourides had created them all with his own blood. The love Dio held for them was infinite.

When Mael finished, he healed the twin wounds, then raised his head. "Thank you."

"Go rest, child." Voice soft, Dio grabbed Mael's arm and pulled him out of the chair, then he took Mael's place. Once Mael left, Dio studied the comatose Nigel for a long moment before he murmured, "What were you doing in that warehouse?"

His Prince of Rome might have been up to no good. It was a hard feeling to dispel. Mael had yet to question why Nigel had been at the warehouse, but Dio had. It was possible Nigel had been kidnapped like Josh and Cian. However, given the elder vampire's dislike of Cian, Dio thought Nigel's motives might have been more sinister.

"Were you trying to rid yourself of a nuisance, Nigel? Must I take Rome from you before you'll stop?"

Because the coma was unlike a natural coma, Dio couldn't read Nigel to get the answers, but he had no problem guessing.

Depriving Nigel of his position wasn't something Dio wanted to do. Did he have any other choice?

An odd scratching sound from the direction of the full length mirror on the wall near him drew his attention. At first he thought Sagan was visiting him again, but the thought fled when Apollonius appeared in the mirror.

Dio rose from his chair, eyeing the gloating vampire. "What are you doing here?

There was no answer from the third formula. When Dio approached, he saw a black wave of energy pour from the vampire. In that split second, he realized Seth was inside Apollonius. Black bolts shot from the mirror and hit Dio before he could raise any alarm.

"You're the only real power they have. Can't have you mucking things up, now can I? Besides I need the little extra boost you will give me. Sweet dreams, Diocourides."

Dio heard Seth as he crumpled to the floor. There was no pain, only the feeling of his consciousness leaving him and no way to stop the drain of his power.

* * *

Every last vampire on the planet had been assailed by the same sense of dread and panic, and all at the same time—right at the exact moment Diocourides had fallen. The severed threads of their connections to their creator had overwhelmed a great many of the younger ones. A large number of elders were acting confused and uncertain, which made matters worse.

The blood Mael had taken from Dio helped counteract the effects. He managed to gather the others into a more cohesive work force. Mael, and a select number of first and second formulas, had been fielding demands to know what was going on since Dio had been found, moments after he'd collapsed on the bedroom floor.

Thank every god in existence Dio had fed him or Mael wouldn't be on his feet now. Everybody who knew the truth had turned to Mael to lead them and fix everything. A very strong sense of his eldest son assailed him, offering strength. Christian's essence, still hidden inside Mael, gave the prince another dose of much needed stability and endurance.

His hands were full with coordinating efforts to find and protect younger members of the Romanorum all over the world. As sunrise crept closer in each region, the calls and demands for help increased. With brutal efficiency, Mael addressed each problem as it cropped up. He wanted casualties kept at a minimum.

"Your second in command, Cornelius, wants to speak to you, your Excellency." One of his assistants held out a phone for him.

Now what? Mael took the phone. "What is it, Corny?"

"Thought I'd call with a touch of bright news in your 'worse than mine' day. We're receiving a ton of reports of weres sheltering our affected vampires until we can collect them. It's made our job a lot easier."

"Our informal alliance with them is paying off. I say it's time to make it official when I return to London."

"I'll talk to Linda about it, oh, happy boss. Corny signing off."

Mael handed the phone back to the assistant. It was a piece of good news he needed in the midst of all the chaos. Darkness formed against a nearby wall, and Mael recognized the first formula, Nikolai. He bowed as Nikolai stepped out from the shadows.

"I believe we can ditch the formalities until this is over, Mael."

"Works for me."

"How is Diocourides?"

Not a flicker of Nikolai's lash betrayed the worry Mael knew had to be beneath the surface. "He's comatose, the same as my father. The magicians are working frantically to find a way to restore his power."

"Xander and the others are on standby. I know Seth has the power to ward any place to stop mental communication, and I've made special arrangements to signal them when we need them."

"I'm going to have to stay behind and handle this. The contingency of firsts and seconds are waiting your command in Diocourides' ward room."

"I left Gabriel and several others handling the problems in their own cities. I don't envy you this task."

He couldn't join Nikolai and the others, and the fear for his angel had increased to more than he could deal with it. For a moment it showed, but he couldn't help it. "Nikolai, my companion's mentor, Michael will take care of Seth. Please make sure Cian is safe."

"I will do all in power to keep him safe, Mael. I promise."

Mael gave him a grateful nod before the first formula turned and headed out to join the elders.

Chapter Twenty-One

Hands still bound, Cian knelt and watched Apollonius pace. Since they'd arrived in the warehouse, the vampire—and no doubt the Egyptian god within him—had been on edge. Cian didn't know what to expect, but he knew Michael wouldn't let him down. He glanced in Josh's direction. The boy had collapsed, but Cian had no idea why. Seth's magic rendered mind speech utterly useless, but Cian constantly relayed Josh's condition to Michael for Dio's sake.

"You're quite the intriguing one," Apollonius said, stopping to stare down at Cian. "I never knew Black had a thing for angels."

Cian gave the vampire a steady, calm glance. "There are many things of which you know nothing."

Apollonius stood once more. "We shall see. I'm surprised you've behaved."

"So long as Josh remains unharmed, I will remain as such."

"Such submissiveness must be a treat for the prince."

Cian smiled slowly. "I'm much more fun when I fight back."

"Oh, I don't doubt that." Apollonius left him and joined the group of vampires who'd entered the warehouse.

Cian counted at least thirty, if not more. If things took a turn for the worse, Cian wouldn't hesitate to guard Josh with his own life. He just prayed Michael got here before that happened.

"I left the idiots enough clues to find us. You'd think they'd have done so by now," Seth, who Cian now recognized had a darker voice than Apollonius, said in an aside to the richly dressed priest near him. "Am I going to have to spell it out for them?"

"My lord," a battle scarred, vampire warrior headed toward Seth. "We've detected a large number of people just outside the perimeter. Equal in number to our own."

"It's about time they got here." He motioned to his own warrior priests. "Stand ready with the vampires. The fun is about to begin."

The formation of men blocked access to Seth and his prisoners. Cian fought the urge to break his bonds. His creator was here, and Cian itched to join him. Duty to protect outweighed all else, however, and he focused his attention on Josh. The young man had succumbed quickly, and it left a knot in the pit of Cian's stomach. He prayed Mael somehow managed to resist

"My lord!" Another vampire threw open the door, then shrieked. A fist broke through his ribcage, the hand gripping his heart.

"Now, now, where's the protocol and formalities?" Seth scowled at the commotion, then grinned when he saw Nikolai at the head of the vampire force invading his warehouse. "Oh, it's you again. Greetings, Nikolai, first formula of the United States."

"Greetings, Seth. Forgive the impetuousness of my comrade." Nikolai dipped his head in Seth's direction.

"Much better. The amenities must be observed, lest we become no more than crass animals. Now, shall we begin?"

One motion of Seth's hand sent a line of fighters forward, weapons drawn. Cian tore his gaze from Josh and Seth's forces and realized the Romanorum had indeed come through. He'd heard about Nikolai, as well as the others behind the man, but he'd never seen them. Beyond the vampires, however, Cian felt another presence. Michael had come, and he waited in the shadows with the rest of the Egyptians. Although he understood their tactics, if it had been him facing the god, Cian wouldn't have hesitated to tear the bastard to shreds

"You always were impetuous," Michael whispered in his mind. *"But you're my general for a reason: you understand strategy. Once the vampires have Apollonius engaged, we will move in and deal with Seth. You remain with Josh."*

"Yes, my Lord."

A flare of energy lit an area behind the front fighters already engaged in hand to hand battle. A second later, the green blast hit Seth but made no impact on the shimmering shield around him

"Oh, you brought toys for me to play with, too. How thoughtful." With a twist of his hand in the direction of the mage, Seth grabbed the vampire from a distance, picked him up, and tossed him against a wall.

A volley of flashing spheres hit Seth's barrier. Hand outstretched, another mage kept up a relentless barrage as he remained behind his own shielding. A momentary rip opened and the ensuing sparks cut Seth's cheek like a knife.

"Very good." Seth smiled in appreciation at the hit. "You didn't do much damage, but it's impressive."

Black mist poured from Seth's hand, directed at the mage. It enveloped him and burnt through his shield like butter. The poor vampire's scream joined the shouts and metallic clangs of swords. The other magicians hit Seth with everything they had.

Spheres of pure power and flashes of electrical currents filled the area around Seth. Nikolai's vampires were fully engaged with fighting Seth's vampires and priests. Blood slicked the floor from multiple wounds.

With Seth and his vampires distracted, Cian snapped his bonds and rushed over to Josh. No one seemed to notice him and he put up his own barrier. He gathered Josh close to him, then shielded the young vampire with his wings. Chaos surrounded them, the entire warehouse a mass of bodies—some moving, some not. He whispered a quiet prayer that Josh didn't wake to this. In the fray, however, he realized Mael and Dio were missing.

Someone walked in a casual stride through one of the doors near Seth, and four others followed behind him. "Haven't you had enough, brother?"

Seth whirled around. For the first time, he looked stunned. "Why are you here, Osiris?"

"We've joined the vampires, Seth. Are you ready to take us on?" A golden man stepped forward, hand held out, palm up. A glowing orb, brilliant sapphire in hue, appeared in it.

"You bastards! You would go against me for them, Horus?" Seth's voice rose in rage, and it fueled the energy he unleashed on the group in front of him.

While the vampires kept Seth's forces busy, Cian focused on the scene unfolding before him. He'd never seen such vehemence, not even from the demons he'd fought. Seth and the other Egyptians hurled their ancient magic, and Cian tightened his hold around Josh. One hit caught Seth and he faltered for a moment. The gods battled with astounding speed, powers colliding into black and golden bursts.

Apollonius and Xander stood transfixed beneath the massive energy forms above them, heads tilted back to see the overhead fireworks display. Lightning streaks from the other mummies joined the golden energy and attacked the barrier protecting Seth and his host. No one as yet had the upper hand.

The noise became near deafening, and the priests still standing stopped fighting. As the lightning flashed around them, they backed off quick as they could. It was clear the battle no longer included them, and they were now frightened. Nikolai leaped into the fray when a group didn't move fast enough to avoid getting hit. One vampire incinerated with no time left to scream. A priest staggered back, bleeding and missing a hand, and another vampire fell to the ground in agony from the burns of the blast. The first formula dragged both men away from the immediate area. Before he could get them to safety, he got caught by flying sparks that burned his face.

Energy spiked sharply in the room and Cian shuddered. He knew that signature like no other. A deafening thunderclap shook the warehouse, and a brilliant bolt struck Seth's barrier. The vampires all scattered as the barrier burst into sparks. Another sphere of brilliant light slammed into Apollonius' chest as the attacker stepped into the doorway.

The black energy body of Seth, entangled within the golden form of Osiris, disengaged, and Seth screamed in shock. He fled back to Apollonius' body in an instant. Flames from the light covered Apollonius before Seth could stop them. He howled in agony, but Apollonius' expression went blank as if no longer in pain.

"This can't happen. I won't let it! Don't leave me, Apollonius!"

Astounded, the other mummies stared at him. Seth was exposed, yet none of them made a move to finish the host body off.

"No, no, no!" Seth screamed. "My brothers, sister, please! Please save him!" Seth fell to his knees, begging them to intervene. "Please, I will leave him. Save him. Don't let him die."

"What the..." At a loss for words, Xander could only stare at Apollonius.

"He's pleading." Stunned, Horus stood indecisive.

"Save him!" yelled Ma'at.

As one, the others threw off their shock. The pulses of their power shifted and warmth suddenly flooded the room. It took all of them to control the damage caused by Michael's power, but they couldn't stop it.

"Michael, please help." Xander, in Osiris' voice, begged.

Michael stood before Apollonius in the blink of an eye. Hands cupping the vampire's face, he entered into what appeared to be a trance. As the fire died out, waves of darkness flowed from every inch of Apollonius' body and into Michael's. Then soothing energy seeped into Apollonius, healing the damage done.

"Do not make me regret this," Michael whispered to Seth's essence.

"Thank you, thank you," Seth muttered repeatedly as Apollonius' eyes opened, not a burn or scar on him.

"Seth?" Apollonius seemed bewildered before he froze at the sight of Michael and the others. There was no answer others could hear, but Apollonius relaxed.

"You have powerful friends." Nikolai commented dryly to Cian.

Cian met Nikolai's gaze as he stood, wings unfolding from around Josh. "You have no idea."

Xander stepped forward and spoke once again in Osiris' voice. "It's time you come with us, brother. There will be no more of this. It's time for us all to heal."

Josh blinked up at Cian, then at the others around them. He looked back at Cian. "Is it over?"

"It's over."

Michael stepped to the side and Apollonius approached Xander. Cian had seen Michael's powers at work many times, but it always filled him with awe. Only then did Cian ask the one question burning in his mind.

"Where is Mael?"

Nikolai answered. "When Diocourides was drained of power, it influenced many vampires, especially the younger ones. The Romanorum has been in a state of chaos, and Mael had to remain there to coordinate the rescue efforts."

"Tell Diocourides we will see him soon," Horus said, then motioned for his family to follow him.

Seth went without argument. Before they left, Seth turned to Michael and spoke quietly, "I owe you more than I can ever repay for saving Apollonius. I swear I will repay the help you gave."

"Leave these people in peace," Michael said. "It's all I ask."

"It will be done," Seth promised before he left with the other mummies. Those of his priests still alive followed as well.

Cian set Josh down, then they joined Michael and the other vampires. The exchange between Michael and Seth might have surprised the others, but it didn't surprise Cian.

Nikolai walked away to coordinate the help for the remaining vampires. He began issuing orders in a voice used to obedience. "Caroline, organize those who can walk to help those who need healed. I want a list of dead before we return to the Romanorum."

"What can I do?" Cian asked.

"Correction." Michael turned to Nikolai. "What can *we* do?"

"You can heal some of the others. Even elders take serious damage from a mummy."

Nikolai had taken a sword hit on one arm as well as some burn damage to his face, but he didn't seem concerned about it. He glanced at Cian, "I take it you can heal, too. I need all the help I can get."

With a nod, Michael went to begin the task of healing the wounded. The energy around him lingered, which startled a few of the more lucid vampires. A simple touch from Michael's hand to each vampire's forehead seemed to ease the anxiety. Pain fled their faces as Michael's magic gently filled them.

"Very few know what I am," Cian said. "Only the oldest truly know what he is."

Nikolai smiled. "At this point, I doubt if many here give a damn."

"Very true." Cian headed for another group of wounded, ready to show the vampires how useful an angel could be.

Chapter Twenty-Two

To those not of their blood, the darkness would have been blinding. To the Black family, however, it was no more than various shades of grey haze. Christian had left his father's body once he'd realized he was needed to protect his blood sibling. He'd reconnected with his body and joined Taylor inside the protection of their family's shadow haven.

Taylor was laid out on a bed made of darkness. Their guardians hovered near both of them, tendrils touching and intertwined with whatever parts of the two bodies they could reach. Christian sat beside Taylor on pillows of shadows and studied the sleeping vampire.

He knew Mael had put Taylor to sleep when Diocourides collapsed. Christian had remained in his father in an attempt to help Mael while he dealt with all the problems. It wasn't hard to feel Mael's worry over Taylor. Taylor had been placed in their shadow home for protection, but the young vampire had never spent any real time within the special darkness. Mael had worried it might traumatize Taylor to wake up there by himself.

The worry brought Christian out of hiding to help Taylor and his father. Mael had enough on his hands without the extra burden. The bedlam reigning in the Romanorum had put Christian's betrayal of his father on the back burner for the time being, but it wasn't far from Christian's mind. He wasn't sure he could ever make up for the damage his silence had caused. Cian had been kidnapped and no one knew if he was dead or alive. How much had his grandfather been behind?

Was he responsible for what happened to Diocourides and Josh? If Nigel was, Christian would be just as accountable.

A groan sound and Taylor shifted where he lay. It took a moment for his eyes to open, but when they did, he sat up quickly, panicked. He looked around, then blinked when he met Christian's gaze. "Chris?"

Relief flooded Christian when he felt echoes of Diocourides return to their proper place inside him. "Hey. Welcome to our secret home."

The surrounding area looked much like an ordinary room except for everything was made of shadows. Taylor seemed to take in their surroundings, then he turned back to Christian. "What happened? Why are we here? The last thing I remember was lying in bed, then it all went... black."

Christian rested his hand on Taylor's shoulder just for the contact. "Diocourides was attacked and drained of power, but I think he's okay now since I can feel him again, and you're awake. Mael was worried about you being alone in here, so I came back to help you."

Taylor rubbed his cheek on Christian's hand, then sighed. "There's more," he said quietly. "I can tell when you're holding back."

"Nigel might be behind all of it. I knew some of it." Christian looked away from Taylor to stare at a distant wall in shifting colors of black and gray. "We still don't know what happened to Cian, and Mael is barely holding on. Only reason he can still function is because he's the one keeping the Romanorum from falling apart."

"Wait. What about Cian? What do you mean no one knows what happened to him?"

"He and Josh are still missing, Taylor. From what I learned from Mael's mind, a large group of our elders were to attack some Egyptian god who was a part of this. Since Diocourides is awake now, maybe they won. I don't know."

Taylor appeared to be lost in thought for a moment. Then he smiled. "Cian's okay. I can feel it." He glanced at Christian. "How are *you* handling all of this?"

"Thank all the gods," Christian breathed out the words in relief. "Mael would lose it if something happened to Cian."

A few seconds of silence lingered, then Taylor cupped Christian's cheek. He started to say something, then shook his head, his smile wistful. "They'll be together soon, and everyone will be happy, right?"

"Yeah, right. I'm sure it will be." He knew he shouldn't, but how could he help himself. Christian turned his head just enough to brush a kiss to Taylor's palm and whispered, "All happily ever after."

"Chris..."

Christian felt lost, only Taylor's closeness keeping him centered. "You and me. We can dream until we leave here. Please?" He turned to face Taylor fully before he pressed a soft kiss to Taylor's mouth. "Let me taste."

"Anything," Taylor whispered. "I'm yours."

The words echoed in his thoughts. Christian parted Taylor's lips with his tongue, the kiss gentle at first. Need rose and hunger followed as his fingers tangled in Taylor's hair, mouth devouring Taylor's. Far from passive, Taylor went from stunned to returning the kiss with equal vigor. A quick flick of his tongue over one of Christian's fangs flavored the kiss with his unique blood. Taylor threaded his fingers through Christian's hair, holding on.

The taste of blood drew a groan from Christian as he pulled away. Eyes closed, he lowered his head, pressing kisses to the line of Taylor's throat until he bit. Mouth tightening, Christian drank what he could.

Taylor gasped, grip tightening in Christian's hair. He shuddered, and a moment later, his wings unfolded and curled around them. "Chris," he murmured, the name followed by an even quieter whisper of 'I love you.'

Christian finally acknowledged the truth. With Taylor came the peace and sense of oneness he needed. Before he stopped feeding, the words echoed back to Taylor. *"Love you, too."*

* * *

It seemed to take forever, but word spread quickly the moment Cian and Josh arrived. When the bedroom door opened, Josh entered first, going straight for Dio. Michael followed him, smiled at Mael, and moved to the side. Cian stepped in the doorway, exhausted but unharmed.

The entire room was filled wall to wall with silent vampires. Mortal news crews had a multitude of cameras pointed at Diocourides. Dio slid his arm around Josh with a smile and continued, "The Romanorum was under attack, but everything is now under our control. There have been numerous vampire deaths across the world, but with the help of our mortal and were allies, the number was kept to a minimum."

The moment Mael saw Cian, the look on his face betrayed the depths of his emotions for his angel. Tension drained from him, leaving a very exhausted looking vampire, but a happy one. He reached out as Cian approached, blissfully unaware of anything or anyone else for just a moment.

Cian drew him close and just held him tight. A few cameras flashed, but Cian didn't move. "I love you so much," he whispered. "I was terrified I might never feel this again."

"You and I both, love. It's been hell." Mael buried his face in the golden hair and nuzzled Cian's neck, taking several deep breaths.

"Our enemy, a rogue wizard, is no longer a threat and has been severely dealt with. There is no truth to any rumors of a rogue vampire situation." Diocourides gave the cameras a confident smile, calm in demeanor and tone.

The story was one Mael had concocted to allow them to deal with the true culprits behind closed doors. It was an entirely feasible one in which Nikolai had gained the cooperation of a cabal of wizards in spreading. Josh clung to Dio, doing his best to match his companion and giving a credible performance.

"How did you ever get through this?" Cian asked quietly. "How did Taylor and Christian fare?"

A long moment passed before Mael lifted his head. "Diocourides' blood and a little help from Christian. I put Taylor in the shadows, and Christian is protecting him. They're both still there. You weren't harmed at all, were you?"

"No, cariad," Cian said, brushing the backs of his fingers along Mael's cheek. "I'm tired in more ways than I can count, but I'm fine. As is Josh."

"Perhaps we should get our children and call it a night." Mael motioned to his nearest assistant. "You're fielding for now. Unless the world is coming to an end, I don't want to know about it until tomorrow night."

"Certainly, your Excellency."

"That's all for now, ladies and gentlemen. I will be holding a special open session tomorrow evening. Roberto will take care of your invitations. Now if you will excuse us." With one last grin, Diocourides waved to the cameras before he dragged Josh off with him.

Cian took Mael's hand. "Lead the way... wherever you hid them."

"I didn't want to take the chance of anything or anyone reaching Taylor." Mael drew the darkness around them, and in the blink of an eye, they were in the specially created haven of his family.

Cian look around, his eyes taking a second to adjust to the utter blackness. Then he smiled when he saw Taylor and Christian. Taylor looked up and his grin widened. Cian went straight to them and hugged them both. "Thank Heaven itself you both are okay."

Christian looked to his father, but only smiled a little. He didn't let go of Taylor's hand, and his fingers tightened instead. "I take it everything is all right now."

"It's safe to return home. The threat is over." Mael slid an arm around Christian's shoulder to hug him, then hugged Taylor.

Cian met Taylor's gaze, then nodded slightly. "We know." He looked to Mael. "We both do."

Christian seemed alarmed.

"Don't worry about things for now, Christian. Everything will take care of itself," Mael reassured him.

Cian chuckled softly. "Relax, both of you. It's not our place to decide whom either of you choose to be with, even if it's with each other."

Taylor squeezed Christian's hand, then lifted it to his lips for a kiss. Christian nodded. The worry faded, but the boy stilled looked grim.

Mael leaned toward Christian and raised his hand to squeeze Christian's shoulder. "I will be at your back, child. Remember that."

There was a perceptible relaxation to Christian's body, and he finally smiled at Taylor. "Do we go back or stay here where nobody can bother us?

"Is it safe?" Cian asked. "You know I'm not much for the throng of mortals clamoring for interviews."

"Only those of my line can get in, and it's very spacious." Mael chuckled. "A shadow mansion."

"I vote we stay." Christian grinned.

One eyebrow lifted and Cian muttered, "please tell me there's more privacy than this."

Taylor barely managed to bite back a laugh. "I'll second that."

When Mael and Cian disappeared, Christian laughed. "I doubt we'll see them for a while."

Taylor cupped Christian's face and pressed a soft kiss to his lips. Then he rested his forehead to Christian's. "Did you mean what you said?"

"Did *you* mean it? You don't even know what will happen to me, Taylor. You sure you want in the middle of it?" Christian closed his eyes, snaking his arms around Taylor.

"With every ounce of my soul." Taylor stroked his fingers over Christian's neck. "Whatever happens, you won't face it alone. I swear to you."

"I think I love you as much as you love me." He opened his eyes to gaze intently into Taylor's. "I know I need to be with you right now, and only you."

"You've got me." Taylor leaned in and kissed him.

* * *

"The rooms are unlimited if you wish." The one they were in was comfortably furnished in varying shades of shadow furniture. It appeared to be a room in black and white, even the paintings on the walls. "It's the safest place in existence for us. There is nothing that can reach us. Except maybe Diocourides since he is the master of all our abilities."

Cian glanced around and nodded. "Lovely place." Then he grabbed Mael's tie and jerked him forward for a kiss.

Mael's laughter was silenced by Cian's hungrily insistent tongue. A deliberate flick of his own added drops of his blood to the kiss as his arms encircled his angel, and they fell back to the softness of the bed behind Mael.

Cian broke the kiss long enough to tug his shirt off. Then he bent for another kiss, fingers deftly undoing the buttons on Mael's dress shirt. He loosened the prince's tie, and when the shirt parted, he ran his hands over Mael. He kissed a path along

Mael's jaw, down the curve of his throat, and finally began peppering his lover's chest with kisses.

Mael soaked in the presence of his lover, focused on every touch, every sound as he ran his fingers through Cian's silky hair. Every sense he possessed was enhanced to take in all he could. His early fears had left their mark, and he twined his thoughts with his angel's out of pure need.

Cian's wings spread out, shielding them from everything beyond the two of them. With every kiss, he poured his soul into Mael. As he moved lower, he caressed his hands along Mael's sides, then down to the prince's hips. His breath warmed the front of Mael's slacks. Mael growled. Now Cian was taking too damn long. Tendrils of shadows shredded their clothing. Once they were naked, Mael rolled them, pinning his angel beneath him.

A deft movement of his hand snatched a small bottle from nearby shadows, and the tendrils opened it for him. He plunged two slick fingers deep into Cian with little ceremony. Cian shouted, eyes widening. Mael stared into his angel's soul, fingers working Cian open. Unable to wait any longer, he withdrew. He pressed the head of his cock to Cian's body, and with one grind of his hips, buried himself deep inside his angel before Cian could draw a breath.

"Mael!" Cian arched, legs locking around Mael's waist. "Yes..." He caught the prince and kissed Mael hard, hips rocking into the unrelenting thrusts.

A surge of Mael's power flooded Cian to reaffirm his presence, and he laid claim to every part of the angel with a harsh demand. The jarring force rocked Cian beneath him, and he moved a hand to Cian's hip, nails digging into flesh. The other slid between them to take hold of Cian's cock. Whether it was the influx of Mael's power, or simply the prince's hand, Cian gripped the man's shoulders and lost the last thread of control. Brilliant light flashed around them, contrasting sharply with the darkness of the shadows. Cian cried out, entire body shaking as he came hard.

Mael struck, fangs burying in Cian's throat. As Mael shuddered with his own orgasm, he drank as much as he could get from Cian. Nothing existed but the two of them and the exquisite pulses of physical and mental pleasure.

It wasn't until Mael licked the wounds that Cian finally opened his eyes. The rest of the space beyond them seemed fuzzy, but he ignored it in favor of staring at Mael's eyes. He still hadn't caught his breath, and given what they'd gone through, he had the distinct feeling it would be quite a while before he could. Cian wanted to say everything that he felt for the man above him.

In the end, all he could say was, "I love you."

Chapter Twenty-Three

Dio had given an open audience session earlier in the day. Everything had been kept calm and orderly for the camera crews and world wide interest. However, his full displeasure was about to be felt. He sat on his throne, gaze pinned on the silent crew in front of him. There was no light-hearted banter this time.

"I want to know everybody's actions in this debacle, and I want nothing left out." He pointed to Christian. "You will start."

To his credit, Christian didn't move under the unpleasant attention. "I knew about my grandfather's plans to drug my father and drain his blood. I also knew about the attack on Cian before it happened. I should have told my father or you, but I didn't." Mael stood on the other side of Christian, arm around his son to reassure him. Christian relaxed as best he could against his father, hand clinging to Taylor's.

Instead of pulling away, Taylor gave Christian's hand a gentle squeeze. "Speaking for myself, I didn't know what was going on beyond my turning. If I had, I would have said something."

"Great Father," Nigel addressed Diocourides with the greatest formality. "He was under threat from me."

"I will deal with you momentarily, Nigel Black." Ice had nothing on the coldness of Dio's tone. "Christian Black, while I may understand the choices you made, I cannot condone them. Under normal circumstances, your punishment would

238

be left to your father, but because of the far-reaching effects, your punishment will be determined by my court."

Mael made a motion for Dio's attention. "Diocourides, I don't wish him punished for his lack of action toward me."

"Duly noted." The chilly gaze moved to Nigel. "Your part in this?"

"I sought to reclaim my blood from my son and to get rid of Cian Carmichael. I also conspired with Apollonius to attack Carmichael." Nigel bowed his head after he finished.

"You are wise to offer no excuses for your actions because I will accept none you would give."

"Diocourides," Cian said. "I wish to make a plea in Nigel's defense."

"Speak if you wish, Cian Carmichael."

Ignoring the myriad looks of utter shock, Cian bowed his head briefly before continuing. "While it is no secret, even to myself, that Nigel despises me, I would like to point out that he is an honorable man when it comes to his sense of duty. When he realized that Josh had been taken as well, he abruptly distanced himself from Apollonius and Seth. In fact, he attempted to protect Josh, and in the end, was greatly harmed himself."

"I will take your words into consideration, Cian. It is very magnanimous of you to speak under the circumstances."

"Thank you, Carmichael," Nigel uttered in a whispering aside to the sorcerer.

"Apollonius, what was your part in this?"

"Diocourides, Apollonius is not mentally stable for the time being. May I speak for him?" The dark energy around the vampire was in full display, indicating Seth was in control.

"You may."

"I accept all blame and responsibility," Seth said. "Apollonius' anger and resentment toward others are what allowed me to coerce him into doing my will. His mind is fragile right now, and... I beg you to spare him. He is not at fault."

Across from them, Triarius struggled not to look away, Lance's hand gripping his shoulder and giving it a squeeze. "Lance and I will attest to Seth's statements regarding Apollonius' mental state. He's been... distant for some time."

"I will leave it to Michael to judge the sincerity of your claims, Seth." Diocourides looked to the archangel to voice an opinion.

"Please, before you speak." Seth turned to Michael. "I address both you, Michael and Diocourides. I have the ability to control Apollonius' instability, and I promise to do so. Neither of us will attempt to harm your kind again. I don't wish to lose Apollonius when I am the one at sole fault for all that occurred. I have come to care a great deal for my host, as I believe he cares for me."

Michael seemed to consider what Seth had said. "I do not condone your actions. However, due to reasons that many do not understand, perhaps beyond Cian, Diocourides, and perhaps yourself, I am able to see through deceit and into one's soul. Even a god's." He turned to Diocourides. "Seth is sincere, and I will attest to the love between them."

Seth visibly slumped with relief. "Thank you for listening to me."

Diocourides paused for the longest moment, gaze traveling then stopping on each guilty vampire as he deliberated what he needed to say. He couldn't allow them to go without punishment. To do so might encourage others to test the strength of the Romanorum.

"Christian Black, I am ordering you to make restitution to those who were harmed over the last month. Not only on a monetary level, but you will personally aid those who suffered. I had in mind to place you in your own city, but you have lost that privilege until you can prove yourself worthy of the honor the Romanorum would place on you."

"I promise I will make it up to you, Diocourides."

Next Diocourides turned to the prince of Rome. "You have disappointed me, Nigel. Your obsession with your own blood line put you square in the middle of this entire mess. It nearly cost us everything. I will not take Rome from you because none of your actions were a reflection on your ability to rule this city. I agree with Cian Carmichael's assessment of you as a man very conscientious of your duty, but you have lost my trust. You no longer have a place in my inner circle until such time as I deem you worthy of my trust."

"I understand, Diocourides, and I am thankful for Cian Carmichael's defense on my behalf."

"You had better be, Nigel, or it will go much worse for you. Do not test me." From the terseness of Dio's words, no one was left in any doubt that he meant it. "Just as Christian must, you will also make restitution for what you have done."

At last he focused on Apollonius. "I am accepting Michael's word for your situation, Seth. If you wish continued freedom with Apollonius, you will agree to your family's monitoring of yourself. I must also command you to make restitution to those harmed by your actions."

"Thank you," Seth said with a bow. "I will do everything in my power to right the wrongs I've committed." Then he glanced at Michael. "Thank you as well. You didn't have to save him, but I'm grateful you did."

"You are welcome," Michael said. "Even gods make mistakes, but we must learn from them when we do."

"For the heroic actions of Cian Carmichael, Mael Black, Michael, and others, the Romanorum will honor their contributions in keeping our institution safe." Dio smiled for the first time and a hint of his mischievous nature shown through in his eyes. "It's party time, boys."

At his motion, the throne room doors opened and a majority of Diocourides' court poured into the room. Loud cheers, calling the names of Mael and Cian, rang forth from the crowd. It was most definitely party time, and the vampires were doing their best to show their support and appreciation for those who had saved them.

Cian bowed to Dio, then turned to Mael. "Is retirement out of the question?"

"London should be a piece of cake after this." Mael hugged Christian against his side before he whispered, "You and Taylor can disappear if you want. Just remember you're returning to London with us."

"Thank you, father. And enjoy the party, you two." Christian returned the hug, then tugged Taylor away with him.

Before they could be overwhelmed, Mael reached for Michael's hand and clasped it tightly within his own. "Words can't convey my gratitude for the help you gave, Michael."

Diocourides joined them, adding his own heartfelt appreciation. "Indeed, Michael. I can't think of a damn thing worthy to do or say in thanks. You'll just have to be immortalized in the best way I can think of."

Michael shook both their hands. "You are most welcome, though dare I ask in what manner I will be immortalized? Humans have done so for eons, and it's amazing how much my appearance seems to change depending on the artist," he laughed.

"Why in Roman fashion, of course: marble." Diocourides chuckled. "There really aren't adequate words, so I'm afraid the marble will have to do."

"Thank you, Michael, and you, too, Cian, for watching out for me." Josh added his thanks in a soft voice.

Michael smiled. "Marble sounds wonderful."

Cian hugged Josh. "There's no need to thank either of us, Josh. You are family."

"I think Dio has a very good idea to thank you, but if you don't want it..." Josh trailed off, waiting for Dio to tell Cian what was in store for him.

"For you, Cian, I got Corny to agree to rule the roost for a month so you can disappear with your prince wherever you choose." Dio winked and grinned at Cian, then addressed Mael. "And Mael, for holding down the fort, you may have anything you want. You have but to ask."

Cian blinked. "By all means... thank me. I think we both need a vacation." He slipped his arm around Mael's waist and smiled at him. "And what would you ask for, cariad?"

"Maybe I'll ask for another month." Mael gave his angel a sly grin.

White mist formed near them, and Selena appeared in all her glory beside Michael. She snaked her arm around her consort's waist. "Are we all happy again?"

Michael leaned down and kissed Selena. "I wondered when you would show up. How are Cornelius and Brandon handling London, anyway?"

"They're plotting the rulers' demises as we speak." She flashed a grin at Cian and Mael. "Honestly, Cornelius is doing far better than I expected him to. Brandon is helping a lot, I'd say. You owe the boy a salary, Mael."

"I already owe Corny a year at his favorite magic shop, but after everything, I probably owe them both a hell of a lot more."

"I'm sure the two of them will think of something," Cian said. "They're dangerous when they start scheming together."

"Maybe they'll want a month off." Mael laughed as he leaned over to whisper something outrageous in Cian's ear, if Cian's expression was anything to go by.

With an insistent look and tug of her hand on Michael's arm, Selena made her wishes known. "I'd say it's time for us to go home. They can handle this world without us for the time being."

"Off with all of you." Dio dismissed them and tucked Josh's arm in against his own. "Maybe I should get a month, too."

* * *

Safely away from the throng of people, Taylor waited until Christian closed the bedroom door. Then he sat on the bed and reached out for Christian. "Join me?"

"Are you sure you want to stay with me?" Christian didn't join Taylor at first. He knew within a few days everybody would know he'd fucked up.

Taylor stood and went to him. He smiled softly, running his fingertips along Christian's cheek. "It's not a matter of whether I'm sure," he said. "Chris, I love you. I can't imagine life without you."

"It's not gonna be easy." Christian closed his eyes at the touch and nuzzled Taylor's hand. "I don't have Diocourides' favor anymore, neither does Nigel. I'd bet money some will make the most of it."

A finger slipped beneath Christian's chin, tilting his face up. Taylor kissed him softly. "But you have me."

Christian melted with the simple touch. "When you put it that way, I don't think I'll need anything else."

Taylor smiled against his mouth, then kissed him again. One hand slipped through Christian's hair, while the other settled at his waist. Christian leaned against him, arms around Taylor's neck. The kiss deepened between them, and he responded to all Taylor gave him. Taylor walked them slowly backward to the bed. He broke the kiss long enough to lie down and pulled Christian down with him. His arms tightened around Christian.

"No matter what happens, don't ever forget that I love you."

"You have my love, too." Closing his eyes, Christian rested his head on Taylor's chest, body curved against Taylor's side. Content after the hell they'd been through, he wasn't going to let go of his own angel for a long time to come. "My own angel," he murmured.

"All yours."

ABOUT THE AUTHORS

Shayne:
She writes, she makes shiny things.

Mychael:
Alter ego of Katherine Cook, Mychael focuses on gay erotic romance stories in many genres. He lives in the eastern US with his family.
https://www.mychaelblack.com
https://www.facebook.com/mblackauthor/

www.ingramcontent.com/pod-product-compliance
Lightning Source LLC
Chambersburg PA
CBHW051637260626
47170CB00004B/1208